BURY HIM DARKLY

JOHN BLACKBURN was born in 1923 in the village of Corbridge, England, the second son of a clergyman. He started attending Haileybury College near London in 1937, but his education was interrupted by the onset of World War II; the shadow of the war, and that of Nazi Germany, would later play a role in many of his works. He served as a radio officer during the war in the Mercantile Marine from 1942 to 1945, and resumed his education afterwards at Durham University, earning his bachelor's degree in 1949. Blackburn taught for several years after that, first in London and then in Berlin, and married Joan Mary Clift in 1950. Returning to London in 1952, he took over the management of Red Lion Books.

It was there that Blackburn began writing, and the immediate success in 1958 of his first novel, *A Scent of New-Mown Hay*, led him to take up a career as a writer full-time. He and his wife also maintained an antiquarian bookstore, a secondary career that would inform some of Blackburn's later work. A prolific author, Blackburn would write nearly 30 novels between 1958 and 1985; most of these were horror and thrillers, but also included one historical novel set in Roman times, *The Flame and the Wind* (1967). He died in 1993.

GREG GBUR is an associate professor of physics and optical science at the University of North Carolina at Charlotte. He writes the long-running blog "Skulls in the Stars," which discusses classic horror fiction, physics and the history of science, as well as the curious intersections between the three topics. His science writing has recently been featured in "The Best Science Writing Online 2012," published by Scientific American.

By John Blackburn

*A Scent of New-Mown Hay**
A Sour Apple Tree
*Broken Boy**
Dead Man Running
The Gaunt Woman
*Blue Octavo**
Colonel Bogus
The Winds of Midnight
A Ring of Roses
Children of the Night
The Flame and the Wind
*Nothing But the Night**
The Young Man from Lima
*Bury Him Darkly**
Blow the House Down
*The Household Traitors**
Devil Daddy
For Fear of Little Men
Deep Among the Dead Men
*Our Lady of Pain**
Mister Brown's Bodies
The Face of the Lion
The Cyclops Goblet
Dead Man's Handle
The Sins of the Father
*A Beastly Business**
The Book of the Dead
The Bad Penny

* Available or forthcoming from Valancourt Books

BURY HIM DARKLY

by

JOHN BLACKBURN

With a new introduction by

GREG GBUR

𝕶𝖆𝖓𝖘𝖆𝖘 𝕮𝖎𝖙𝖞:

VALANCOURT BOOKS

2013

Bury Him Darkly by John Blackburn
First published London: Jonathan Cape, 1969
First Valancourt Books edition 2013

Published by Valancourt Books, Kansas City, Missouri
Publisher & Editor: James D. Jenkins
20th Century Series Editor: Simon Stern, University of Toronto
http://www.valancourtbooks.com

Library of Congress Cataloging-in-Publication Data

Blackburn, John, 1923-
Bury him darkly / by John Blackburn ; with a new introduction
by Greg Gbur. – First Valancourt Books edition.
pages cm
ISBN 978-1-939140-17-3 *(acid free paper)*
1. Mystery fiction. 2. Horror fiction. I. Title.
PR6052.L34B87 2013
823'.914–dc23
2013004079

All Valancourt Books publications are printed on acid free paper
that meets all ANSI standards for archival quality paper.

Design and typography by James D. Jenkins
Set in Dante MT 11/13.5

10 9 8 7 6 5 4 3 2 1

INTRODUCTION

WHEN beginning to read a John Blackburn novel, it is almost impossible to predict what sort of story one is in for. What usually starts as a single murder or strange incident may spiral into a sinister conspiracy, a worldwide pandemic, the rise of a demonic cult, a new horrifying phase of human evolution, the awakening of a slumbering monstrous god – or worse. Of his works, it is fair to say that Blackburn's 1969 novel *Bury Him Darkly* may be the oddest and least predictable of them all. A crude assassination segues into the search for the lost treasure of a madman and, eventually, to a deadly secret hidden for centuries.

John Fenwick Blackburn (1923-1993) had an eclectic upbringing and early life that is an appropriate fit for his unpredictable storylines. He was born in Corbridge, Northumberland, England as the second son of Charles Eliel Blackburn, a clergyman who provided a stern and presumably rather unhappy childhood. Older brother Thomas would turn to alcoholism later in life, but John would find an outlet in writing about the darkness of humanity. Before this, however, he began his academic studies at Haileyburg College in London in 1937. His education was interrupted by the onset of World War II, and John served in the Mercantile Marine from 1942 to 1945 as a radio officer. At the end of the war, he completed college at Durham University, earning his bachelor's degree at the age of 26. From there he became a school teacher for several years, working in both London and Berlin. During his time teaching in England, he met his future wife Mary Joan Clift, and they were married in 1950. When Blackburn returned to London in 1952, he became the director of Red Lion Books. His writing began while running the bookstore, resulting in 1958 in the immediately successful horror/espionage thriller *A Scent of New-Mown Hay*. Blackburn decided to leave Red Lion and devote himself fully to his writing, though he and his wife jointly managed an antiquarian bookstore on the side.

Blackburn's personal life informs much of his writing, and he even goes so far as to give characters the surname "Fenwick" after himself in several books. He and his brother shared an interest in hill climbing, and climbing plays a key role in a number of novels. His 1963 thriller *Blue Octavo* is centered in the world of antiquarian bookselling, a subject that Blackburn was well-versed in. Sailors and onboard ship life are also featured in a number of books, including his premiere *A Scent of New-Mown Hay.*

It is evident that Blackburn's personal fears also inspired his work; an astonishing number of his plots are based upon the threat of a deadly disease. The only modern comparison is screenwriter/ director James Cameron's obsession with nuclear weapons, which are present in most of his earlier films, including *The Terminator, The Abyss, Aliens,* and *True Lies* (not to mention *Terminator II*). In the 1950s, though, there were plenty of other things to worry about, and Blackburn exploited these fears in his writing as well. The memory of the Second World War and the horrors the Nazis had perpetrated were fresh in the public consciousness; also, the Cold War was burning bright and communism cast a long shadow over the free world. Both groups would feature prominently and regularly in Blackburn's novels, most often as villains, but some-times in a more ambiguous role.

This description may give a misleading impression that Black-burn was unimaginative or repetitive. On the contrary, each of his novels is centered on a particularly clever, even diabolical, idea, and it is arguable that Blackburn's reuse of villains or threats freed him to focus more on the central conceit.

This brings us to the story of *Bury Him Darkly.* Blackburn introduces the reader to the legend of Martin Railstone, an 18th century painter, author and scientist who was either a genius or a madman – or both. A mediocre thinker for most of his life, Rail-stone entered a mysterious period of brilliance in his old age, and spent the last fifteen years of his life working in seclusion. Nobody saw the fruits of his labors: Railstone ordered that his works be buried unseen with him in an intricate and secure custom vault constructed under Caswell Hall, his old home. He left bizarre and seemingly impossible conditions in his will allowing for the tomb to be opened again only upon the appearance of a blood relative of very specific physical characteristics.

Under the control of the Anglican Church since Railstone's passing, Caswell Hall is now in imminent danger of being forever lost, as the valley containing it is due to be flooded in the construction of a new dam. This threat spurs an eclectic group of individuals to band together to rescue Railstone's legacy before it is too late, each of whom has his or her own motivations for entering the tomb. Lord Marne, a ruthless self-made millionaire industrialist, views the opening of the tomb as a personal challenge. His compatriot George Banks is obsessed with uncovering the lost art and writings of Railstone. Marjorie Wooderson, who wrote Railstone's biography *A Light at Midnight*, imagines the man a neglected genius and she is eager to see her views vindicated. Erich Beck, a professor of bacteriology and former Nazi scientist, curiously believes that Railstone had made scientific discoveries of importance to modern medicine. Mary Carlin, a local lecturer in history, cares nothing for Railstone but believes that the tomb may contain an ancient religious artifact. Reporter John Wilde is simply looking for a good story.

This odd collection of personalities must overcome an array of obstacles to reach their goal: not only political resistance from the church, but also dangers in the wickedly constructed tomb. Will any of them be truly prepared for what they find when they reach Railstone's body and his legacy?

Many of Blackburn's novels feature stock characters as the heroes, such as the aging but astute General Kirk and the brilliant, egotistical bacteriologist Marcus Levin. *Bury Him Darkly* is quite unusual amongst Blackburn's novels in that it not only does not feature any of the regular cast of characters, but it does not even have a clear protagonist for most of the story. Part of the fun of the book is trying to figure out who, exactly, will step forward to save the day.

In general, "fun" is really the word that comes to mind when trying to describe Blackburn's writing. His books are all fast-paced, carrying the plot along effortlessly and without any unnecessary filler. The stories carry enough twists and turns that it is almost impossible to predict the conclusion. None of his novels are more than 200 pages, or roughly 70,000 words, in length, and all therefore make for a fast and thrilling read. I have found it genuinely difficult to put down one of his books once I've started. My impression from reading many of them is that Blackburn had a true love of writing, and his enthusiasm crosses over onto the page.

Bury Him Darkly was positively received by critics of the time. Writing in the May 17, 1970 issue of *The New York Times*, crime fiction reviewer Allan J. Rubin said, "This is another of Blackburn's gripping, elemental confrontations of good and evil." Paul Robbins of UPI penned a review, printed in the September 14, 1970 issue of the *New Castle News*, which concluded, "The cast of characters falls in line with the bizarre plot. The yarn ends just about the only dramatic way possible. Creepy." The October 16, 1970 issue of the *Scottsdale Daily Progress* includes a review by Bradley Simon that suggests that "this novel of suspense, horror, occult, science fiction, or mystery (the reader's choice) lives up to the author's usual standards of excellence."

It can be seen from the latter review that even some of the reviewers didn't know quite how to describe *Bury Him Darkly*. This raises an interesting question: what, if anything, was the inspiration for Blackburn's truly bizarre tale of buried secrets, mad geniuses, and an elaborately constructed tomb? Blackburn himself does not seem to have spent much time discussing the origins of his ideas, so any explanation of them is mere speculation. When I first read *Bury Him Darkly*, however, the story sounded oddly familiar; this has led me to my own hypothesis of its genesis, which I now share.

In 1795, so the story goes, 18-year-old Daniel McGinnis saw mysterious lights on the uninhabited and remote Oak Island in Nova Scotia. Visiting the island soon after, he found a strange circular depression in the ground and a tackle block hooked to one of the trees, suggesting a recently refilled excavation. As this was still in the era when piracy existed in the Americas, McGinnis considered the possibility of buried treasure. He and two friends returned to the island and dug to a depth of 30 feet, finding layers of logs placed every ten feet down.

This trio did not continue their search, but a legend was born, and the Oak Island "Money Pit" would draw in investors and treasure hunters almost continuously through the 19th and 20th centuries; in fact, excavations are still ongoing today. Millions of dollars have been sunk into the search, making the name "Money Pit" appropriate for more than one reason. The mystery apparently deepened in the 1850s, when the pit – now dug to a depth of 90 feet – flooded to the 30 foot level and could not be bailed. Investigations suggested that the water was flowing through man-made tunnels from the island's beaches, which were also apparently engineered by the pit's designers to siphon water to it, a "trap" for would-be excavators. Enthusiasm for the treasure hunt only increased with such discoveries: clearly *something* important must be buried on Oak Island, if someone went to such trouble to hide it! The pit drew worldwide attention: in 1909, future President Franklin D. Roosevelt was an investor in the pit, and in 1939 King George VI was apprised on excavation progress.

So, if something was concealed in the Money Pit, what was it? And who built the pit? Oak Island is perhaps unique among treasure hunts in that neither of these questions have answers. The most popular theory is that the island served as a treasure depository for a pirate such as Blackbeard or Captain Kidd. More unusual is the idea that Marie Antoinette's lost jewels were spirited away to the island after the French Revolution. Even more bizarre is the notion that the Knights Templar – crusaders in the Middle East from the 12th to 14th centuries – hid the the Holy Grail in the pit!

Most peculiar of all theories, however, is the idea that the Money Pit contains the lost writings of the English Renaissance man Francis Bacon (1561-1626), who among other things concealed evidence that he is the true author of Shakespeare's plays! This hypothesis was first advanced in the 1953 book *The Oak Island Enigma* by Penn Leary. Bacon was a philosopher, scientist, author, statesman and jurist of quite high regard for most of his life, and is noted for being an active advocate for the scientific method as it is known today. He fell into disgrace in 1621 when he was accused of, and confessed to, corruption in his legal doings, and he spent the rest of his life relatively isolated, focused on his writing and research.

With this "Bacon theory", we can see many similarities between the Oak Island story and that of *Bury Him Darkly*: a brilliant man of antiquity, who falls into disgrace and isolation, who constructs an elaborate trapped resting place for his lost wisdom, waiting for the time when someone sufficiently enlightened can claim it. The "Bacon theory" is what came to mind when I first read Blackburn's novel.

Of the "true" story of Oak Island, it is important to note that almost all of the "facts" of the story have been called into question. The first account of the pit appeared in print in the 1850s, long after its supposed discovery in 1795. Geologists have concluded that the flooding of the pit is most likely a natural phenomenon and not an elaborate trap, and the artificial nature of the beach is also suspect. Nevertheless, treasure hunters have remained undeterred, in spite of the great cost in money, time and, occasionally, lives.

In 1965, four years before Blackburn's *Bury Him Darkly* would be published, the Money Pit made international news when four men died in one of the many shafts dug on the island. Treasure hunter Robert Restall was overcome by fumes when he descended into the pit and suffocated; his son and two others died attempting rescue. The fumes may have come from one of the pumps used to fight the constant flooding. News of the tragedy made it to London, where it appeared in the August 17, 1965 issue of the *London Times* with the terse title, "Four treasure hunters die."

If this story had captured Blackburn's attention, a little searching would have readily turned up a 1965 story about the Money Pit in *Reader's Digest*, which also mentioned the theory about Francis Bacon's writings. Blackburn may have been intrigued by the idea of different groups of people searching for a treasure of unknown nature, each with their own imagined idea of what rested within the pit.

Could the Money Pit have formed the genesis for Blackburn's *Bury Him Darkly*? As I have said, this is only a hypothesis, and Blackburn's inspiration will, like the nature of the Money Pit itself, likely remain a mystery. In any case, I believe readers of *Bury Him Darkly* will find that John Blackburn has written a story that is more unusual and compelling than the most fevered dream of any treasure hunter.

GREG GBUR
January 29, 2013

BURY HIM DARKLY

For James Smyth

Preface

'WHAT a grand evening for it.' The car had topped a rise and old Dan Gorman beamed at the rolling landscape spread out before him. To the left lay fields of young corn, to the right open downland, while straight ahead the towers of Lanchester cathedral were soaring out of the horizon like the sails of a square-rigged ship. 'Have a swig of whiskey just this once, Fergus.' Dan reached in the glove compartment and held out a bottle of Donegal Dew bearing the slogan *Not a Drop for You till I'm aged Twenty-Two*.

'I'd best not, Dan.' Fergus O'Connor shook his head reluctantly and his hands remained on the steering wheel. 'You know I try to keep off the hard stuff while we're working, though I must say I could do with a bit of Dutch courage today.'

'Don't worry yourself sick, me boy.' Dan raised the flat bottle to his own lips. He had had three drinks previously and they and the beauty of the landscape were giving their blessing to the enterprise. 'A good and most reliable man the client has shown himself. Didn't he pay the first instalment cash on the nail and supply us with every possible detail we needed? Hasn't he promised faithfully that there'll hardly be a living soul anywhere near the cathedral because it's the last day of the annual regatta and everybody will be down by the river?' Both men considered the package which had been handed over to them in a Dublin pub three weeks ago and contained two pages of typed instructions, one thousand pounds in worn fivers and the promise of a further thousand when the job was completed to the client's satisfaction.

'Yes, all by the river except the feller we're meeting, Fergus. Very regular in his habits the good gentleman is. Whenever he's in residence, he tries to get back to his house – palace I should say, of course – by seven fifteen. Wet or shine the chauffeur drops him in the street and he takes a stroll around the cathedral before having his supper. Nice that, Fergus. Communin' with nature one might suppose. Sure, there'll be no difficulty about the job at all.'

'It's not the job I'm worried about, Dan.' Fergus glanced at the dashboard clock and increased their speed very slightly. 'We've been in business for over thirty years now and we're about the only real professionals left. But we've never been asked to do business with a clergyman before.'

'Oh, don't let's go on about that, boy.' Dan smiled at his partner with deep affection, the sunlight glinting on his false teeth and the gold watch chain draped across his ample belly. He was fat and Fergus was thin, but they were both dressed in identical black serge, wore bowler hats and quiet ties. Their expressions were alike too; mournful and humorous and slightly shady and they might have been two cynical undertakers anticipating a profitable epidemic.

'This feller is not a proper clergyman at all. All he's got are Anglican orders dating from that old ram Henry the Eighth and quite invalid. "Invincible Ignorance" is the kindest excuse for him.' Dan had deserted Mother Church long ago, but still held strict views on heresy. He replaced the bottle and unfolded the map which their client had thoughtfully included with his instructions.

'Fork left at the roundabout and left again at the end of Queen's Crescent. Ah, but it's a lovely peaceful place, Fergus, and quiet too, as we were promised. I can almost feel the Grace of God flowin' around us.' He grinned with appreciation as the car turned into a long Regency terrace and the cathedral loomed up before them. The regatta was one of Lanchester's main events and the town was almost deserted.

'That's it, take the next fork and park at the end of the square, Fergus.' Dan lit a cigarette, still smiling at the scene around them. Smooth lawns led down to a stream flecked with swans, the cathedral walls were mellow in the soft evening light and its green roof blended with the sycamore trees surrounding the precincts.

'They say that after Durham, Lanchester is the finest example of Romanesque architecture in Europe.' Dan had been studying a guide book to while away the journey from London. 'Building was started by Henry de Tourville in 1073 and the main structure completed during the reign of Edward III. It was damaged by a bad fire in 1521 and knocked about by Cromwell and the Puritans, may hell remain hot for the bastards.' He glanced at his watch as the car drew up, leaned back contentedly and started to hum an I.R.A. ballad.

'On the eighteenth day of November
Just outside the town of Macroom,
The Tans in their big Crossley tenders,
They hurried along to their doom.'

'If only I had Dan's nerves.' Against his better judgment Fergus reached for the bottle. As he had said, he hardly ever drank when they were working, but this was a very special job and he had to steady himself. But as he gulped back the whiskey, the smooth mellow liquid appeared to have no power in it and the car clock was racing before his eyes.

'For the boys of the column were waiting
With hand-grenades primed on the spot,
And the Irish Republican Army
Made balls of the whole bloody lot.'

'For Christ's sake, Dan, will you stop that?' For the first time in years Fergus snapped at his friend and, high above, the cathedral clock struck the quarter and confirmed his anxiety. 'I'm not worried about the man's profession now, but look at the time! Regular as Epsom Salts he's supposed to be, so what's holding him back? Once that regatta's over the streets will be jammed tight.'

'Ease yourself, boyo, and don't worry. The regatta will not finish till eight and the reverend gentleman is obviously taking a little longer over some charitable work. He'll be along directly. – But look at them two mots, Fergus.' Dan pointed at two mini-skirted girls crossing the far corner of the square. 'Jesus, what a feast of entertainment God gave to men with really filthy minds.

'What did I tell you? Here comes his lordship to keep the appointment, just as the client said he would.' An old black Daimler had turned out of a side street and was trundling sedately towards them. Fergus switched on his engine and they both smiled; Fergus with relief, Dan with humour.

'Ah, a fine democratic feller, he must be, riding up there along with his loyal retainer.' A uniformed chauffeur was at the wheel of the Daimler, and a small figure with a shock of white hair just visible between a clerical collar and a wide-brimmed hat, was perched beside him.

'Good evening to you, me lord, though we'd expected you to be dead on time. What have you been up to then? Why do you require our services, I wonder? Still, that's not our business and we're happy to oblige.' Dan chuckled as the Daimler stopped, a door opened and the white-haired man stepped out. He wore a dark suit, and a silver cross gleamed against his chest. After a few words to the driver, he closed the door and the big car turned and moved away down the street.

'He's a fine little chap, Fergus. Dudley Lanchester, Lord Bishop of the Anglican Communion, once a sportsman of some note and now considered a sort of saint, so I've heard. Let's go and meet him.' The gaitered legs were walking briskly towards them as their owner made his way to the cathedral grounds, and Fergus slipped their car into gear. 'You're not still anxious, are you?'

'No more, Dan. The whiskey's started to work and it's just another job, like you said.' Fergus's feet hovered on the clutch and above the accelerator. 'That's it, your lordship. Stop and look up at the rooks as we were told you would. I was getting a bit worried about him, Dan. Dangerous things are motor vehicles and I thought the good old gentleman might have gone and met with an accident.' His feet moved in unison and the car shot forward.

Dudley Renton, Bishop of Lanchester, had removed his hearing aid after saying good night to the chauffeur and he neither heard nor saw death hurtling down on him. He was still watching the rooks circling the cathedral towers when the bumper caught him and the wheels and chassis ripped the life from his frail, old body.

'No, not quite dead on time, Fergus, but as near as makes no difference.' The car drove on towards the London road, Dan Gorman glanced back, took a leisurely pull at the whiskey and resumed his humming.

> 'And the Irish Republican Army
> Made balls of the whole bloody lot.'

One

BISHOP RENTON had been a popular figure and he was deeply mourned. At his funeral, the Royal Family were represented, two archbishops conducted the service, a Roman Catholic cardinal read the lesson, and the coffin was borne by six sporting personalities, including the captain of the Australian cricket eleven.

On the day following his death, the morning papers gave him the full treatment. 'BISHOP OF LANCHESTER SLAIN BY HIT-AND-RUN DRIVER.' 'TRAGIC DEATH OF CHURCH LEADER.' 'GRAVE LOSS TO CHRISTIAN UNITY.' 'FORMER ENGLAND CRICKETER KILLED.' Those were a few of the headlines and George Banks smiled happily as he read them.

'An act of God.' Banks was a small, unobtrusive man in appearance, but his eyes could become overbright and overexcited at times and he muttered his feelings aloud. 'Yes, I can see God's hand clearly.'

The middle page of the *Daily Globe* carried a photograph of the dead divine and a three-column obituary, because Dudley Renton had been in the news for most of his adult life. All-round sportsman with three Cambridge blues and eight Test series to his credit . . . Advocate of Anglo-German friendship in the 'thirties who had become disillusioned during a visit to the Fatherland and soundly denounced the Führer to his face . . . Rich young man who had quite literally sold all he had and given it to the poor . . . Missionary, imprisoned and tortured in China . . . Crusader for Christian unity . . . Television personality. Renton's full life was laid out in glowing terms, but George Banks glared at the thin, academic features as if they belonged to anti-Christ.

'A terrible thing, Mr Benks. If I had my way, those hit-and-run drivers would be treated the same as murderers.' Banks's secretary breathed heavily over his shoulder. 'And to think that if he hadn't left that regatta early to take his regular stroll in the cathedral grounds, he'd still be alive. Almost a saint, my Mum thought he was. Said that half an hour of the bishop on the telly gave her more comfort than the whole Bible.'

'Renton was good according to his lights, Miss Thornton. But he was also a deluded, superstitious fool and a stumbling block in the path to human knowledge.'

'Really, Mr Benks. I'm surprised you can say such a thing about the dead. Everybody knows that Bishop Renton was a very learned man indeed.' Gladys Thornton made no attempt to conceal her distaste and once again considered asking for a transfer back to the typing pool from which she had only recently been elevated. Nobody was overworked at the Ministry of Rural Development, their department was probably the slackest in the building, and Gladys, who thought and talked in clichés, considered her job a piece of cake. All the same, she frequently remarked to her colleagues, and to her Mum, 'Mr Misery-My Banks gives me the creeps,' and ' "It's a sad heart that never rejoices." '

But he was rejoicing now. He was beaming as he pushed the paper aside and rubbed his little pink hands together in glee. 'Yes, that was the man's public image, Miss Thornton. That was the impression he gave to the uninformed. In reality, Renton was a bigoted enemy of art, literature and learning. For years we have pleaded with him, grovelled before him and he would not yield a single inch. Now, at long last, he is out of the way and the road will be open for us.'

'*We*, Mr Benks? Us? You mean the Ministry grovelled to him?' Gladys frowned for a moment and then her face cleared. 'Oh, you're talking about that society you belong to. The Caswellites?'

'That is the abbreviation, Miss Thornton. Our full title is The Adherents of Sir Martin Railstone and the Openers of the Caswell Tomb.' Banks frequently rebuked Gladys for mispronouncing his name, which he suspected she did deliberately, but today he was in too good a humour to bother. 'For over ten years our society has been pressing for the vaults at Caswell Hall to be opened and the paintings and written works Railstone placed there to be brought out and given to humanity. The educated public have been on our side, the law has offered no objection. Only the Bishop of Lanchester has held us back and now, at last, the obstacle has been removed.'

Banks considered those years; how he had first opened a copy of

Railstone's *Inner Darkness* and heard his hero speak to him directly; how he had been browsing one day in the National Gallery and wandered by chance into a room of Railstone's landscapes. A man with few friends, Banks was never lonely or bored because he had a purpose in living; and, as he bent over the newspaper again, he prayed that Renton's killer would go undetected, as appeared likely. Two girls returning from the regatta had seen a car parked near the cathedral shortly before the bishop's body was found, but they had not noticed the occupants, the number plates, or even the make, and that was all the police had to go on.

'I've heard of Railstone, of course, Mr Benks. Seem to remember that we did him at school once. Wasn't he known as Little Boy Blue or the Caswell Vampire?' Gladys considered that the Caswellites were just the type of society Mr Misery-My would belong to: a bunch of loonies who wanted to open the tomb of an eighteenth-century nobleman who had been potty himself.

'Yes, Miss Thornton, those were the names his uneducated contemporaries called him. Railstone was a small man physically, and he suffered from dropsy and a skin complaint which gave him a very dark complexion. All the same, he was one of the greatest men humanity has ever produced, my dear.' It was the first time Banks had used an affectionate term to address his minion, but he was very happy indeed. D Day was almost there. Soon the seal would be broken, the stone rolled away and the faithful would enter the vaults to bring Railstone's works into the light of day.

'Have you read *Sonnets to Martha* or *The Inner Darkness*, Miss Thornton? Have you seen the "Dream Landscapes" in the National Gallery? Read him, my dear, look at his paintings and you may start to share my enthusiasm. But Railstone was more than just an artist or a man of letters. He was an historian as great as Gibbon, a scientist who may have anticipated the discovery of bacteria by at least a hundred years and, towards the end of his life, perhaps a prophet.'

'Yes, it's coming back, Mr Benks.' Gladys recalled her schooldays and a series of textbooks which all contained the word 'notable' in their titles: *Notable Men of Letters*, *Notable Statesmen*, *Notable Explorers*, *Notable Scientists*. Most of the series had been as dry as dust, but the editors had allowed a certain levity in *Notable British Eccentrics* and the reader was regaled by the antics of such personages as James Boswell, Squire Mitton and the Rector of Stiffkey. She could clearly recall an illustration of Martin Railstone, blue-faced and red-haired, gazing down into the tomb which was to receive his body.

'Wasn't he a bit funny towards the end? You know what I mean, Mr Benks.' Gladys tapped her forehead. 'Weren't there stories that he was looking for perpetual motion and the Philosopher's Stone? That he was possessed by the Devil and had murdered a lot of women?'

'Lies put out by the envious and believed by the superstitious, Miss Thornton, and I would be glad if you would try to pronounce my name correctly.' Though Banks resented the word 'funny' he could not bring himself to be really angry, because the Promised Land was clear in sight and nothing else mattered. All his life he had been a follower of illusions and lost causes. The quest for Martin Railstone was by far the most absorbing of them.

'For fifteen years up to the time of his death, Sir Martin did not publish one book or exhibit a single canvas, though we know he was working hard. He told his closest friends that he was busy on a line of scientific inquiry so startling that it must be kept from the world till humanity was ready to receive it. In his will he included a quotation from Saint John's gospel: "I have yet many things to say unto you, but you cannot bear them now."'

'Did he indeed!' Gladys was a firm believer that the Devil could quote scripture for his own ends, and there was no doubt that Railstone had been a devil, whatever Misery-My might think. 'And all those pictures and books were buried with him, Mr Banks?'

'Correct, Miss Thornton. Those were his instructions.' Banks lit a cigarette. He usually rationed himself to two with a glass of beer in the evening but it was a day of celebration. 'Think of it, my dear. Fifteen years' work by a man of genius buried beside his body in the Caswell Vaults. Paintings and great writings and scientific theses mouldering away in a tomb. They are our goals, Miss Thornton, what we have been fighting to recover, Railstone's last and probably greatest works which must be given to the world.'

'But if he himself said they were to be locked up in the vault, I don't see what can be done about it.' Gladys looked at Banks's bright, flickering eyes and then at the office clock. He really was quite potty on the subject and it was time for coffee in a few minutes. Her friends from the pool would have a good laugh when she told them.

'Everything will be done, Miss Thornton.' Her superior got up and paced pompously across the room like a lecturer before his class. 'Martin Railstone made a will within a week of his death and he was not a sane man when he made it. The great mind had broken down at last and the very thought of dying appears to have obsessed him. For several months workmen had been preparing a tomb beneath his home, Caswell Hall; an immensely strong chamber which was to house his body and a chest containing all his later works. Yes, he was clearly insane at the end. The very wording of the will proved that.' Backwards and forwards Banks paced the floor with his chest stuck out, his hands clenching and unclenching and his voice loud with excitement.

'"In that sealed tomb, my body and my works must lie undisturbed till a red-haired woman of my blood and my two physical infirmities . . ." he suffered from dropsy and a skin complaint, as I told you . . . "is found to claim them."

'Railstone's only relative was an unmarried sister, already middle-aged at the time of his death, and he must have known such a person would never exist. The clause is meaningless – the product of a sick mind; a final joke before the death-bed. The lawyers are agreed that the will should be disregarded and the tomb opened to recover his works and from all over the world eminent persons are demanding it.' Banks halted by his desk and frowned at the newspaper photograph of Dudley Renton.

'Only that man stood in the way, because the will, made when Sir Martin was no longer in command of his faculties, also directed that Caswell Hall and all his fortune should be held in trust by the Diocese of Lanchester till the appearance of that red-haired female who could not possibly exist. Over and over again, Lord Marne, the president of our society, had begged that the vault be opened, but always the bishop refused him.

'Now, now at last, because of one careless driver, the stumbling block has been removed and we shall have our way. The Dean and Chapter are bound to be reasonable and very soon the world will know what a genius Martin Railstone really was.'

'That will be very interesting, I'm sure, Mr Banks.' Gladys had looked at the clock again. 'But do you see the time? Eleven fifteen and we're due for our coffee break. All right if I pop down to the canteen?'

'Of course you may.' Banks suddenly remembered that he had a private telephone call to make. 'And don't hurry back, Miss Thornton. I won't need you for at least half an hour.' He picked up the instrument as she walked out of the room and asked for an outside line.

'Lord Marne, please. George Banks here.' A switchboard answered, then a secretary told him to wait and it was a good five minutes before Marne's voice greeted him.

'A very good morning to you, George. I presume that you have been reading the papers and are calling to say how happy and excited you are that Dudley Renton has returned to his Maker and the last barrier is down. Or would stumbling block be a more appropriate term? I have heard you use it several times in the past.' Desmond Marne, self-made man, Doctor of Science, millionaire industrialist, had a thick Belfast accent with the hint of a sneer in it.

'Quite so.' He put up with Banks's enthusiasm for exactly twenty seconds and then broke in abruptly. 'As it happens I heard the news at nine o'clock last night and, as President of the Society, rang the Dean shortly afterwards. He is a new man, as you probably know, only appointed a few months ago, and hardly in the picture at all. Though naturally distressed by the bishop's death and pitifully ignorant on the subject of Railstone, he appeared a reasonable enough fellow and told me that he had no personal objection to the tomb being opened, providing there was no legal difficulty and that it was done in a reverent manner.'

'This is wonderful, sir.' Banks could not contain himself. 'Until Renton's successor is appointed, the Dean and Chapter are in charge of the diocese and all we need is their permission. Now at last . . .'

'Please listen to me, George.' Marne had not made his fortune by suffering fools gladly and his sneer was much more apparent. 'Till recently I felt much the same as you do, but now matters have changed completely. The stone has not been rolled away from the tomb, the seal is still unbroken, as Marjorie Wooderson poetically put it in her biography of Railstone. And there is every possibility that it will remain unbroken for ever.

'I said listen, man. The Dean telephoned me back less than half an hour ago and his attitude has changed. It appears that while going through Renton's files he came across a certain document which distressed him deeply. He now refuses to allow us to open the tomb and we shall have to wait till a new bishop is enthroned.'

'That should not take long, sir.' Banks smiled as he interrupted. 'Renton was a fanatic where Martin Railstone was concerned. He believed all those slanders about murder and black Masses and alchemy. He considered that Sir Martin was possessed by the Devil and, during a death-bed repentance, ordered his works to be buried with him because they were evil.

'But Geoffrey Brownjohn, the Archdeacon of Bylden, is bound to be appointed to the bishopric. You told us that yourself, sir, at the last general meeting. Brownjohn is not a superstitious fool. He is a most reasonable man who won't put any obstacles in our way. We have waited so long. What do a few weeks, or months, matter?'

'You mean that you don't know, George?' Marne gave a low whistle of astonishment. 'You have not realized that our time is running out? Haven't you heard of the Cass River Scheme? Well, for your information, it is being prepared by your own ministry and if the project goes through quickly we may never have a chance of opening the Railstone tomb, because Caswell Hall will be at the bottom of a reservoir. The odds are that Brownjohn will have been enthroned long before that, of course, but we are not out of the wood yet. In fact the trees are closing in on us. I would study the details of the Cass Scheme, if I were you. To the best of my memory the reference contains the initials K.V.I.' There was a click and the line went dead.

*   *   *

'Yes, indeed, all my original brain-child, Banks, though our political masters will claim the credit, of course.' Mr Kingsley Virgil
Isaacs was of a higher civil service grade than Banks and he had
a large room facing south and wall-to-wall carpeting to prove his
superiority. He also had a big metal drawing-table, and he beamed
at the maps and papers spread out on its surface.

'Still, creation has its own rewards and one mustn't grumble.
Once I was told to draw up plans to flood the valley and form a reservoir, I decided that only the latest civil engineering techniques,
recently developed in Italy and Germany, could be used.' Mr Isaacs
was a product of Haileybury and Oxford, but he originally hailed
from Trinidad, and he unrolled a map with blue-black fingers.

'You are an architect, so you'll be able to appreciate that the
scheme is quite brilliant, though I say so myself.' Isaacs inflated his
chest proudly as he bent over the table.

'The Cass Valley is entered by seven streams which meet here
to form the lake and the river, and both the eastern and northern
slopes are natural watersheds. But this is where the real beauty,
the simplicity, of my plan lies.' A second map, showing layers of
geological strata, was spread out.

'These two ridges at the southern end of the depression are
rock, solid Portland stone, which not only form a bottleneck but
will provide me with natural foundations to build on. Easy as falling off a log, as they say.' For no apparent reason, Mr Isaacs gave a
belch of laughter and dealt his guest a friendly pat on the shoulder.
He had rowed for his college and still boxed heavyweight for the
Ministry: the blow almost knocked Banks off his feet.

'All we need to stopper our bottle is a lightly constructed dam,
seven hundred and forty feet long by twenty feet high, and there'll
be no expensive excavations to worry the Minister. Just remove
the top surface here, do a little blasting here and here, and we
build right on top of Old Mother Nature herself. Sections of pre-
cast concrete supported by steel buttresses will be quite adequate
because the foundation is so solid, and there will be no pressure to
speak of.' He pushed a series of drawings towards Banks.

'The maximum depth of the lake is to be twenty fathoms and the average depth only two. Sounds footling, but with the whole floor of the valley under water, we'll have a capacity of well over a hundred million cubic feet. Ample for the new industrial centre they've built at Thornhanger and more than a drop left over for Portsmouth and Southampton. Clever and cheap, eh? The whole construction shouldn't cost more than a million and a half; not allowing for pipe-laying or any external work, of course, and by using prefabricated sections for the main structure the work can be rushed through in record time.' Isaacs shook his head and lit an evil-smelling cigarette which Banks suspected might be a reefer.

'A brilliant plan, as I'm sure you'll agree. But who'll take the credit? Not the designer, K. V. Isaacs, M.SC., M.I.C.E., A.R.I.B.A., who did all the work. Some puffed-up little trade union leader who can't tell a hawk from a hand saw.'

'But how far has the scheme got?' Banks stared hopelessly at the drawings. Caswell Hall would lie at almost the deepest point of the reservoir and be buried under more than a hundred feet of water. Less than fifty yards from his own office Isaacs had been working out his abominable plan, and he had not even heard about it.

'There must be masses of red tape to be got through before you even ask for tenders. What about the purchase of the land and planning permission, to start with?'

'Nothing to worry about there.' Isaacs' huge white teeth opened and another bell-like laugh reverberated around the room.

'They must have water for Thornhanger New Town, and the Minister himself has given his blessing. Tenders for the work and the reinforced sections are already in and, between the two of us, the contracts will go to Spender-Wade of Tyneside and Heldmann of Essen, who have suitable sections in stock. As for getting hold of the land, we won't even need compulsory purchase orders. The valley belongs partly to the Ecclesiastical Commissioners and partly to a number of small farmers, and they're all bending over backwards to sell out. The area is damp and rocky, useless for agricultural purposes though ideal for the reservoir, as I have shown you.

'Strangely enough, we did have a slight panic this morning, as it happens.' He dealt the map a sharp rap on the site of Caswell Hall. 'A fellow called Lord Marne, who represents some crackpot society, telephoned and claimed that this house should be preserved as an ancient monument and also because it was the home of a minor poet whom nobody reads today – Hailstorm or Brainstorm; maybe Gallstone. I'm not sure of the name but I remember it was a damn silly one.'

'The name was Martin Railstone and I and a great many other people read him, Mr Isaacs.' Banks fought back his irritation.

'Do you indeed?' Isaacs had no eyebrows to speak of, but he raised what he had. 'I've little time for light literature myself; only worker bee in this hive of drones.

'In any case, Marne's complaint will cut no ice at all. The house has little historical or architectural interest; just an Elizabethan manor, built over some Norman ruins and in a sad state of neglect. As for the bard, Rainstorm, the Minister has not even heard of him. Added to that, this section of the valley belongs to the Church and they're clamouring to exchange contracts. A hard-headed bunch when it comes to business, these clerical gentlemen. Richest corporation in the country, so I'm told. I'm a Liberal Fundamentalist myself; senior elder at the Duke Lane Chapel in Putney.

'But just a moment. You live in Putney, don't you?' His eyes glowed with brotherly love and welcome. 'Do come and join us one Sunday. You'll find we're a very friendly bunch.'

'Thank you, Mr Isaacs. I'm sure you are.' Banks had no interest in Isaacs' religious activities and his heart was racing as he stared at the maps and drawings which could destroy a dream. 'How long will it be before they start work on the dam?'

'That's hardly for me to say. I'm just the poor bloody designer. But Spender-Wade are brisk operators and the Germans have the sections on hand. We'll have to get finished before the weather breaks and the streams start to fill up, in any case. At a very rough estimate I would say that the valley should be under water well before the end of October.

'But what's the matter, old man?' Isaacs studied him with sudden concern. 'Feeling ill? You look all green and shaky. Here, try one of these, man.' He opened a packet of cigarettes stated to be Player's, though the limp brownish cylinders bore no resemblance to the advertised product. 'Best pick-me-up there is.'

'No, no thank you, Mr Isaacs. I am perfectly well and most obliged to you for the information, but I must get back to my office now.' Banks winced as one vise-like hand crushed his palm while another pounded his shoulder and he lurched down the corridor as though he were drunk. Isaacs' estimate of six months was probably over-optimistic, but how long would it take to appoint a bishop? For over two hundred years those priceless treasures had been buried in Railstone's tomb and it almost appeared that the Fates were plotting to keep them buried.

But there had to be a way. If only a few manuscripts could be produced, if one painting were recovered, the world would cease to jeer at the society and the Dean and Chapter would be forced to open the vault. He had thought of Renton's death as an act of God, but it had signified nothing. All the same, God acted through men as well as by miracles. As the thought occurred to him, his steps grew firmer, his expression of worried misery vanished, and his face became hard and purposeful.

George Banks was the most law-abiding of men, and his life had been completely uneventful. But his troubled mind suddenly told him that he was a chosen instrument to carry out the divine will. Lord Marne and the Society might wait in the hope that the new bishop would be appointed soon, but he, George Banks, had finished with waiting.

He strode into the office with high heart, nodding curtly to Gladys, and sat down at his desk feeling like a true man of action with a great challenge before him; Hannibal surveying the Alps, Ulysses outside the walls of Troy, Drake viewing the Pacific Ocean.

The decision was made and the die cast. Before a week was out he intended to enter the tomb of his hero.

*   *   *

On the surface George Banks and Lord Marne had little in common. Physically Banks was small and insignificant and usually passed unnoticed in a crowd, while Marne had a battered face which looked as though it had been carved out of a block of oak and an aura of vitality which made him the centre of attraction wherever he went. Socially and financially they had no links either. Banks had attended a minor public school and held a not very important position in a minor governmental department, while Marne had fought his way up from a Belfast gutter to the control of an industrial empire which he ruled with a mixture of ruthlessness and charm.

Also, on the surface Marne was a jovial and kindly man, generous to dependants and popular with his equals. A man who could be relied upon to be a good friend provided things went his way. Frustrate him, however, scratch that surface, and the veneer of jollity and good fellowship vanished to reveal a second personality which was quite different; a completely unrelenting individual without mercy or compassion who would stop at nothing to gain his own end. Though he had lost his religious faith years ago, during his teens Desmond Marne had led a street gang, known as the Sons of King James, which had terrorized the Protestant population of Belfast. Two men still bore the marks of his razor, and the body of a woman who had informed against him was buried somewhere up on the hills behind Larne.

But beneath that second shell of cynicism and ruthlessness lay the core of his character which united him to George Banks, because Marne, like Banks, was also a dreamer: the Celt who had wept over the sorrows of Deirdre, the altar boy who had felt a personal and physical triumph at the culmination of the Mass.

Those things lay in the past, and for a time nothing had taken their place: no love of women, no children, and once his financial future was assured, even the fun of business went out of his life. He had tried many substitutes: travel, collecting art treasures, archaeological expeditions to the Middle East and Mexico. These last had been the best of his interests, but they hadn't really absorbed him. Then, three years ago, the story of Martin Railstone had started to fascinate him and the opening of the tomb had become a personal challenge.

The strangeness of the man's verse and his paintings had been the first things to arouse Marne's curiosity, and when he had studied the three biographies of Railstone and learned of the chest of pictures and manuscripts that were supposed to have been buried with him, he knew that it was his charge to recover them for himself and mankind, however great the cost. Within a week of coming to that decision he had joined the Caswellite Society, and slowly but ruthlessly the more flamboyant cranks and eccentrics had been weeded out and the hierarchy filled with people as efficient as himself. To Marne those hidden treasures in Caswell Hall had become a quest and an obsession, and he intended to see that they did not remain hidden much longer. Renton had stood in his way, and Renton was dead. He was quite sure it would take far more than the Dean of Lanchester to stop him.

There was plenty of time, too. He had spoken as he did to George Banks because he believed that anxiety was an excellent quality in inefficient subordinates, and Banks's lack of information had infuriated him. But the Dean's change of mind had not worried him in the least. The man had claimed that a certain disturbing document, written by Railstone, had come into his hands, and had tried to persuade him that the vaults should remain closed. The Dean's opinions were unimportant. His friend, Archdeacon Brownjohn, was certain to succeed to the bishopric and Brownjohn had promised that one of his first acts would be the opening of the Caswell vaults.

Marne hummed to himself and crossed to the window to draw back the curtains. Long flat clouds were drifting beneath the moon to throw shadows across the downs, and the slopes dominating the Cass valley were just visible in the distance. Marne had bought the house eighteen months ago on a sudden whim which he had felt he might regret. But he had no regrets now. Whenever he drove down from London he had a feeling of home-coming; he was returning to the country of a man whose story and works fascinated him. Martin Railstone might have been insane or possessed, as many of his contemporaries had considered likely, but Marne knew him to have been a genius. Before the first bulldozer arrived to start work on the dam, the tomb would be opened and the fruits of his genius made public. He inflated his chest with the cool night air and strolled across to a telephone that had started to ring.

'Good evening to you, Geoffrey.' He smiled as he heard Brown-john's voice. 'Does this mean that you've had confirmation – that the appointment is definite?'

'Not actually, Desmond.' The Archdeacon sounded ill at ease. 'Oh, there is no doubt that the bishopric would be mine for the asking, as they say. But the fact is that something else has cropped up and I won't be coming to Lanchester after all.'

'Something else? I'm afraid I don't understand you.' Marne's grip tightened round the instrument. 'You said that you were bound to succeed Renton.'

'So I was, Desmond, but I don't want to now. I've always thought of myself more as a scholar than a churchman, and just this evening – a few minutes ago – I had some wonderful news. They've offered me the Chancellorship of Salisbury University, and that's exactly the sort of job I've been longing for. Aren't you going to congratulate me, Desmond?'

'Congratulate you for breaking a promise?' Marne spoke very slowly and deliberately. 'Listen to me, Geoffrey. You have to come to Lanchester. I need you here. Without your help there is a grave chance that the Railstone legacy may be lost for good. You must succeed Renton.'

'No, I'm sorry, but it's out of the question. I do appreciate your feelings about Caswell Hall, but you should try and understand my point of view. At Salisbury I will have enormous opportunities for research and study. That book on the Coptic liturgies I have been planning, for instance . . .'

'Is that important enough to make you go back on your word to a friend?' Marne's feelings were a mixture of impotence and fury. He had always considered Brownjohn a pliable nonentity, but the worm had turned with a vengeance. 'To break a promise?'

'I made no promise, Desmond. I merely said that if I were ever appointed Bishop of Lanchester, I would order the opening of the vaults. I shall not be appointed bishop and I must tell you that I am quite determined to go to Salisbury.'

'Then there is nothing more to be said. Goodbye, Geoffrey.' On Marne's thirteenth birthday, two much older boys had tried to take a cricket bat away from him. Both of them had ended up in hospital. Now, as he replaced the telephone, his face bore much the same expression as when he had raised the bat and clubbed his first assailant in the teeth.

Two

IN the distance the Cass Valley had looked a lush and friendly place: a wide saucer of cultivation set in a fold of the downs, and one wondered why there were no villages, no farmhouses and so few grazing animals. Then, as the road wound down from the north and Lanchester Cathedral sank behind the hills, the truth became apparent. What had appeared to be tilled ground was bog and moorland and clumps of willow herb and bracken, and the few animals were small black-faced sheep quite out of place in southern England. The Cass Valley was a wilderness of marsh and rock and stunted trees; a freak of nature which one might have expected to find in Scotland or North Wales, but certainly not within ten miles of the English Channel. Almost in the centre of the valley lay the lake, with Caswell Hall to the right of it: a long crumbling Elizabethan manor house that seemed to crouch miserably in a hollow like some trapped animal waiting for the hunters to put an end to its tortured life. Even George Banks had to admit to himself that Mr Isaacs had been right in choosing this place as the site for his reservoir.

'Apart from the foundations, this hallway is all that remains of the original Norman structure.' The guide had a Sussex burr which must have been incomprehensible to some of his listeners, but George knew his lecture by heart. Only conducted parties were allowed into the house and he had heard the man half a dozen times already.

'As I have told you, the Benedictine Monastery was founded by Abbot Vulfrum in 1076. The abbot's body is buried in Lanchester Cathedral, but in this niche to my right stands his likeness. You can see that it has been much mutilated, probably during the reign of Henry the Eighth when the monastery was destroyed and the site became the property of the Railstone family, who built the present structure.' He pointed at the stone figure of a monk set into the wall. One arm and much of the face were missing, but a single eye and what was left of the mouth showed an expression of cold disdain.

'Yes, the abbot looks a bad-tempered old gentleman, doesn't he? Lived to be a very great age and was a friend of both William Rufus and the Usurper, Stephen. Rufus stayed at the monastery on several occasions and there are tales of orgies and other goings on to be found in local folklore. Knowing the Red King's reputation I shouldn't think any ladies took part in those orgies.' He wagged a finger at his audience. 'But then I mustn't say anything about that, must I? It being all legal and above board nowadays.

'Historians are divided about Vulfrum. Some consider him to have been cruel and avaricious and others a most misjudged man who sheltered the poor during the wars between Stephen and Matilda. But those were troubled times and not much accurate information is available. "The years when God and his saints slept," as they'll have told you at school, my dear.' He beamed at a small child who was chewing toffee as a cow chews cud, and motioned the party to follow him.

Half past four. George Banks glanced at his watch. For another thirty minutes he would have to endure the guide's boring, inaccurate rigmarole and listen to his jokes and blasphemies. Still, this was the last tour of the day and once the visitors had left he would be able to carry out his plan. The haversack on his shoulders might look half empty but the weight of the chisels and hammer and crowbar it contained felt strangely reassuring. He was a qualified architect and for more than a month he had been studying the layout of the building; its strength and, above all, its weaknesses; the way into the vaults where knowledge and great art lay buried. He grinned to himself as he followed them through the gloomy rooms and corridors. Caswell Hall was not so much a show place as a curiosity for the morbid-minded and was in a terrible state of disrepair, with sagging floors and peeling plaster. Now and again through an empty window frame came the sound of heavy diesel engines. Mr Isaacs' plan was already in operation, and the contractors were bringing up their equipment to erect the dam.

'There is the great hall of the Elizabethan building which was completed in the same year as the Armada, though the carved ceiling was added by the notorious Sir Martin Railstone about whom I shall have a lot to tell you. The design is supposed to depict the interior of a whale, as seen by Jonah, and there is not a single piece of metal in the entire structure.' The guide raised his arm impressively. 'Every joint is dowelled.'

'Cor, but it's cold in 'ere, Mum.' The cud-chewing child clutched her parent's hand. 'I don't like it in 'ere.'

'Very, very cold, isn't it?' Their instructor jumped at the cue. 'A lovely warm day outside, but we might be locked in a refrigerator. Many other people noticed that, ladies and gentlemen. When the house came into the possession of the Diocese of Lanchester in 1770, they tried to use it as a seminary for young clergymen. But did it work? Not for a moment. Neither staff nor students could live here. They said the cold and the sad atmosphere of the place froze 'em in their beds. The same thing happened when it was let out to private families. Time after time they packed up and left and the house has been empty for over fifty years now. What is the reason for it, I wonder? Is Martin Railstone's body still alive in that grave, perhaps? Does his ghost walk through the corridors at night, as some people think?

'Just you come down from there, lads.' He raised his voice at two youths who were halfway up the staircase. 'Them stairs are full of worm and wood rot and we don't want any accidents.

'Yes, Sir Martin Railstone, ladies and gentlemen. A great poet and artist, they say, though I've never been able to understand his work myself. Also a man of science. His book *The Sceptical Philosopher* is highly prized by collectors of medical material.

'But what else was he, I wonder. Are those stories mere legends invented by superstitious peasants, or did Sir Martin indeed gain his creative talents by selling his soul to the Devil? That empty room on your right was said to have been used partly as a chapel and partly as a laboratory. Did Railstone really kidnap those unfortunate women and sacrifice them to his master on the stone table you can see by the window? No, not that room, sir. The one over there.' Again the man raised his voice. This time to George, who had turned away in disgust.

'Whatever the truth, towards the end of his life Martin Rail-stone's reputation became so unsavoury that he was feared throughout the county. Few servants would work for him, and to complete the tomb which I shall show you in a moment he had to import foreign craftsmen from Italy. We are told that he was hard at work to the time of his death, but he did not make public one painting or poem.' He paused dramatically before moving to open a door at the far end of the hall.

'We will now visit the ante-chamber to the vault, the strang-est room in this very strange house. But Sir Martin was a man of perverse humour and I would advise those of you in charge of children or of a squeamish disposition not to approach the actual tomb too closely. Now, now, madam, there is no need to push.' Like a sheepdog penning an unruly flock he allowed them to pass one by one through the doorway.

The room was approximately twenty feet square, with a stone floor and ceiling, and it was illuminated by three stained-glass win-dows depicting Percival's quest for the Holy Grail. In the centre of the floor stood a massive iron cage with bars reaching up to the ceiling. There was a second door in the opposite wall and George stationed himself beside this, trying to appear bright and inter-ested though he had come to regard the guide, whose name was Smith, with deep personal loathing.

'We are now in the ante-chamber of the tomb, ladies and gen-tlemen. It was built by Italian workmen, as I told you, and the bars of the cage are no less than three inches thick. The lock to its door is just as formidable and has never been opened in two hun-dred years.' The lecture droned on while streams of coloured light flowed from the windows to give the room an almost fairground effect.

'On the evening of Good Friday, seventeen hundred and sev-enty, an old manservant of Railstone's called on the Lord Bishop of Lanchester, Dr Henry Dayten, and handed him two documents. One appears to have been a private letter which Dr Dayten did not make public, and the second was Railstone's will.

'In this testament Railstone put all his fortune in the care of the diocese, with instructions that not only his body but also a chest containing all his more recent paintings and manuscripts should be placed in this prepared vault and the entrance sealed. The seal was to remain unbroken till a certain event took place: an event which he must have known was most unlikely to occur, ladies and gentlemen. The discovery of a female descendant who possessed his colouring and was cursed with his afflictions. You will remember that Railstone suffered from dropsy and had vivid red hair and a dark skin which earned him the nickname of Little Boy Blue.

'Well, what could Sir Martin's motives have been? That is the question which scholars have been asking over the generations. He must have realized that such a woman might never exist, so why enter such a meaningless condition? Was the clause a senile joke? Was the man insane? Or was Dr Dayten's theory correct? Had Little Boy Blue made that pact with the Devil and repented when he knew death was approaching? Did he fear that his body might return to life and attempt to break loose, like some Frankenstein monster, to trouble the earth? Does that chest contain a record of Railstone's dealings with his terrible master?' The time for gratuities was drawing near and Smith gave his audience the full treatment, shaking his head, rolling his eyes and gripping the bars of the cage.

'Was it that pact, that repentance, that fear of resurrection which caused him to build this structure and place the house in the safe keeping of the diocese?

'Look at the workmanship, ladies and gentlemen. Three-inch bars of iron set in the floor and ceiling, a solid block of basalt, a lock with a single key that has always been kept by the bishops of Lanchester in person. What was the reason for such precautions? To prevent anyone robbing the tomb, or to stop something coming out?' Smith grimaced, gave another long, slow shake of the head and produced an electric torch from his pocket.

'Within a few hours of Dr Dayten receiving the will, Railstone died and his orders were obeyed. He was buried darkly by candlelight, the chest was placed beside his body and the vault sealed. Most probably it will remain sealed till the end of time, because the valley should be under the reservoir before a new bishop is appointed. Little Boy Blue lies beneath us, his secrets guarded by

iron and rock and very soon water may provide them with a third
guardian.

'Now, if the children will remain where they are, I will show
something interesting to the adults. No, just you stand still, little
girl. You'll know what it's all about when you're a bit older. That's
right, Madam, come close to the bars.'

This was the moment George Banks had been waiting for. Last
week he had oiled the lock and hinges of the second door and the
key was hanging from a nail in the wall. While Smith shone his
torch into the interior of the cage and the visitors gave the custom-
ary chorus of 'Cor's and 'Oh's and appreciative titters, he fitted the
key into the lock.

'Yes, ladies and gentlemen. I said that Sir Martin was a man of
perverse humour and that is his last joke.' The beam of the torch
lit up a rampant bronze phallus standing almost upright in the
centre of the slab like the boss of a shield. 'Only a very peculiar
mind could have chosen such a monument, and the inscription
beside it is equally curious. As you can see it is written in Italian
and may be translated as follows:

'"A Red King found Me.
A Dead Priest Bound Me.
A Usurper Feared Me. Martin Heard Me.
But Whence Comes She who can Deliver Me?"

'Well, what does that mean, I wonder. Scholars consider that the
Red King, the Priest and the Usurper must refer to Rufus, Abbot
Vulfrum and Stephen, who are all associated with this house, while
Martin is obviously Railstone himself. But what the whole jingle
signifies, and who the mysterious Me and She are, is pure guess-
work.' Everybody was leaning far forward now and George made
his move. The lock turned, the well-oiled hinges moved soundlessly
and he stepped out into the sunlight, closing the door behind him.

In medieval times the monastery had been surrounded by a
moat and, though the water had been drained off centuries ago, a
ditch choked with bushes and small trees remained.

The door opened out on to a causeway, but George ignored
this and scrambled down into the depression to study the founda-

tions of the building, which formed its inner bank. If he had approached from the grounds he might have been spotted and he wanted to make an entrance by day in case torchlight revealed his presence. He felt that he had planned for everything and, as his trained eye examined the wall before him, he realized that his task would be even easier than he had expected. After the monastery was dissolved the solid facing blocks had been replaced by bricks and knapped flints, and time had increased their several weaknesses. Behind that frail barrier lay the tomb of his hero, saint and demi-God, and before long he would be standing inside it. In a few minutes work could begin. Through the chink of the door he heard the guide finishing his discourse.

'That concludes your visit to Caswell Hall, ladies and gentlemen, and I hope it has whetted your curiosity. The mysteries of Sir Martin's life and death and strange burial are fully recounted in his biography by Marjorie Wooderson, which may be purchased at the lodge for thirty-five shillings; a most entertaining and also scholarly work, as I'm sure you'll agree when you've read it.

'Ah, thank you very much, sir, I don't mind admitting that gratuities are deemed a part of my stipend. Thank you too, sir. That's most kind of you, madam. Mind the uneven floors in the corridor – and no skylarking from you, me lads. As I've said before, there's a lot of woodrot in the building and we don't want any accidents.'

George listened to the party shuffling away and then unslung his haversack and opened the flap. It only contained tools at the moment but soon, very soon, it might carry away a painting and a manuscript executed by Martin Railstone. George felt enormous self-confidence as he drew out a hammer and chisel. Everything was going to go as he had hoped, and he had no fears of interruption. Once the visitors had left, the guide would follow his regular routine of locking the house and outer gates and settling down with his wife to high tea and an evening of television. A formidable barbed-wire fence surrounded the grounds, but George was provided with cutters to take care of that, and his car was parked down the road. Already he could see himself standing before Lord Marne and the other members of the society and proudly revealing the first gems from the treasure trove.

'The first brick is the worst brick.' That was a maxim he had once heard from an old mason and he laid the chisel carefully into position and started to drive it home with the club hammer, still feeling a sense of self-confident exhilaration as the mortar crumbled and broke up beneath his blows. When he was a boy George had longed and pleaded to enter the priesthood, but his father, a hard-headed country architect, had forced him to follow his own footsteps. Now, swinging the hammer, watching the brickwork crack and shatter, feeling his chisel loosening the whole course, it really appeared as if he was working under some divine inspiration. A few yards away from him lay the works of a God-given genius, and God himself had ordained that he recover them for mankind.

There was the first brick disposed of at last. He laid down his tools at the sound of voices and motor vehicles starting up as the trippers flocked away. His several visits to the Hall had given him Smith's exact timetable. Already he would have locked the door of the house; it would take him three minutes to secure the outside gates and another two to reach his lodge and retire for the rest of the evening.

George smiled smugly to himself as he waited. He knew exactly what people thought about him: that he was a nonentity to the widowed sister who kept house for him, a gloomy bore to the office staff, and a neurotic to his doctor. Yet it was he, George Banks, who had been given the courage and will power to take action. When he had first suggested breaking into the vaults to the society, they had all sneered at him. Their view was that the only remaining obstacle was Bishop Renton, and once he died or retired they would have their way. Lord Marne had appeared angry at the very thought of such an illegal act, and had also stated that the task was impossible because the walls of the house would be too solid to cut through without special equipment.

How wrong they were. As soon as he resumed work George knew that the whole wall was rotten. After the Dissolution the facing stones of the monastery had been carted off to be used in other buildings, and this was soft Tudor work. At each thud of the hammer, a brick moved and mortar cascaded down into the ditch.

To have attacked the vault from above – cutting through the bars of the cage, raising that deeply-cemented slab of basalt – would have been an impossibility. All he had to worry about was bringing a mass of loose stuff down on top of him.

Even in that God was helping him. The ditch was littered with dry timber, much of it sound, and close to hand lay a piece of the exact size he needed for a lintel. George fitted the branch into the opening he had made and started to attack the next course of brickwork, while high above martins and swallows darted to and fro, curlews swept across the slopes of the valley and an old bald crow stationed itself in a nearby thorn tree and occasionally croaked hoarsely as if in answer to the sound of his hammer.

The wall appeared to be composed of three thicknesses of brickwork packed with rubble, and in the centre he had to go carefully. The packing was loose, merely held in position by its pressure against the bricks and, though he could pick out the lower strata easily, there was no means of shoring up what was out of reach. Now and again, he had to draw back hurriedly as rumbles heralded a cascade of broken stone and pebbles, and his right hand was bleeding from a deep cut when he finally cleared the second cavity and stood back to survey his handiwork.

Yes, that must be the last thickness of bricks and the courses were much tighter and more professionally laid than those he had already penetrated: probably eighteenth-century work supervised by Railstone himself. The sun was still high in the sky and the day had been very warm when he had started work. But though he was sweating freely, George felt a sudden spasm of cold as he took a torch from his haversack and studied the packed arches of rubble above him. They looked safe enough, but he'd have to go carefully because undue vibration might produce an avalanche. He also had a vague but uncomfortable sensation that he was being watched.

The sun on his back was warm and comforting, and for a brief moment he thought of abandoning his work and taking a rest. Then he shrugged and pushed aside his anxieties. Only four inches should lie between him and his goal, and he hoped to be through them while daylight lasted. He selected a finer chisel and started to attack the inner wall.

This was good, honest brickwork put up by men who had intended the structure to last. No weather had penetrated the narrow joints of rich, well-mixed mortar and it took him a long time to make any impression on them. He worked very carefully, now and again glancing nervously up at the tons of rubble suspended above his head, and all the time the sun sank lower in the west. But his hammer rang steadily on, inch by inch the chisel cut into the joints, and finally he had a purchase to lever out the first brick.

He was through and nothing else mattered. That narrow opening he had made led straight into the vault and his calculations had been entirely correct. George had no thought of falling masonry now, he no longer glanced up at the hanging rubble, and he wasn't even curious enough to take his torch and shine it through the opening. He knew that some great power was helping him, guiding his hand on the chisel, strengthening the blows of the hammer, leading him to the weaknesses in the cement. He whistled as he worked and brick after brick made way for him, some coming loose so that he could draw them out intact and others breaking into fragments that rattled on the floor of the vault. Two cross bearers broke up and a large section came away in one piece, so that he almost believed the wall itself had surrendered to him. The hammer rang merrily on and his blackened face was a mask of elation. The prince who cut through brambles to release Sleeping Beauty could not have worked more eagerly than did George Banks.

At last he was about to claim his reward, to bring evidence to the world and prove what a great man his hero had been. He laid down his tools and took the torch from his pocket. The breach in the wall was far larger than he needed to crawl through, but somehow it appeared important that he should approach Railstone's body upright and with dignity.

He lifted the torch, seeing the opposite wall of the vault some fifteen feet away from him, and stepped through the gap. Brick rubble crunched under his feet, another spasm of cold racked him, but no cobwebs clutched at his face, there was no smell of damp or rot, and the torchlight lit up tiles that looked as hygienic as the floor of an operating theatre. Another step and another crunch of rubble, a third step forward and the sun was behind the valley now and the torch was the only light he had.

The fourth step and then no light at all. The torch had dropped from his hand to shatter the bulb on the floor and George Banks screamed. He screamed to drown the noise which had broken out on every side of him and he swung wildly around in horror, his flailing arm striking something that felt warm against the general coldness of the vault. He stumbled back towards the opening, pressing his hands to his ears, and terror and a purely animal urge to escape were his only emotions.

Sir Martin Railstone was dead. He had died two hundred years ago and his body had rested undisturbed in a vault of thick brick-work and sealed by rock and metal. But in that vault somebody was alive. Somebody was laughing in great, roaring, bellowing gusts of mirth that echoed around the walls with a threat and a sneer and a promise in them.

Three

' "When paupers die only the louse and flea do mourn them,
  Worms rejoice.
  If tyrants go their halls are filled with weeping for a span,
  Then with mirth's voice.
  But I fear not the common fates of man,
  Fire, water, earth.
  I shall lie quietly waiting till you come
  To bring my second birth." '

The words reverberated loudly round the room, but there was a deal of scorn in the reader's voice and he closed the book with a snap.

'Do you call that literature, Lord Marne? I should have said it was composed by an imitator of John Donne – and an incompetent and unbalanced imitator, to say the least.' The Dean of Lanchester, the Right Reverend William Norseman, D.D., D.S.O., M.C., pushed aside

the copy of Railstone's *Inner Darkness* and transferred his attention
to a Mayfield Press edition of *Dream Landscapes*.

'And I am afraid that it will take more than these meaningless
daubs to persuade me to change my mind.' He flicked quickly
through the plates and then leaned back and lit a cigar.

'I am the mildest, the most patient of men, ladies and gentlemen, but I will not be coerced and your persistence has begun to
provoke me. Irrational, irresponsible, illogical: those are the words
I must use to describe your efforts to open that tomb and whitewash
the memory of a thoroughly depraved human being.' Norseman
was getting into his stride. He weighed seventeen stone, most of
them bone and muscle, towered six foot three from his great black
boots to his closely-cropped grey hair, and was referred to by his
subordinates as the 'Bison' with no apparent affection.

'But perhaps you are labouring under a misapprehension, my
friends. Perhaps you imagine I am a modern, South Bank Churchman who does not believe in evil and can turn a liberal eye on the
abominations of Martin Railstone's life.' He shook his head very
slowly and took a pull at the cigar.

'If so, you are most sadly mistaken. I do believe in the divinity
of Jesus Christ, Lord Marne. I do believe in the Virgin Birth and
the Resurrection, Mrs Wooderson. Had I the slightest doubts on
those matters I would immediately resign my orders and cease to
obtain money under false pretences.' Before taking up his present
appointment three months previously, Norseman had been Chap-
lain-General to Her Majesty's Forces and he glowered at his guests
as if they were a parade of defaulters.

'I also happen to believe in diabolic possession, Professor von
Beck.'

He blew cigar smoke across the table and considered each of his
guests in turn. Lord Marne, who looked more like a professional
wrestler than a highly qualified chemist and wealthy industrialist.
Marjorie Wooderson, the author of *A Light at Midnight*, that trashy
and sentimental biography of Railstone. The reporter John Wilde,
who appeared half asleep, had hardly spoken a word so far, which
was at least one thing in his favour. Mary Carlin, a history lecturer
at the local university, looked a pleasant and intelligent girl, so why

had she got herself mixed up with such a bunch of cranks? Finally the German, von Beck: it was amazing that a man with his record had dared to show his face in England. If that Nuremberg tribunal hadn't been so chicken-livered they'd have strung him up before he could say 'Heil Hitler'.

'When you telephoned me shortly after poor Renton's death, Lord Marne, I said that I would give your request my sympathetic consideration. That was because I had been only a short time at Lanchester and knew little about Martin Railstone. But now . . . now I know a great deal about Railstone and I can tell you this.' A gnarled fist beat the table top in emphasis. 'As long as I am in charge of this diocese, the Caswell vaults will remain closed. It may well be that a bishop sympathetic to your aims will be appointed before the valley becomes flooded and, in that case, I would have to stand aside. But I want to make my present position completely clear to all of you.'

'So you have done, Mr Dean. Abundantly clear. But may I ask why you changed your mind so suddenly? When I first telephoned you, you were most sympathetic and then, almost overnight, your views had altered.' Marne smiled, his Irish brogue was pleasant and friendly, but underneath the smile he was fighting to control his anger. He had sworn to discover what the vaults contained and the bishop's death should have removed the last obstacle. Now Norseman had entered the fray to frustrate him.

'What was the real reason, sir? Did your colleagues advise you to refuse my request? Was it out of respect for the late bishop's opinions? Or was that mysterious document the only motive force?'

'I have already told you that that was the case, Lord Marne,' Norseman replied with a gruff bellow. 'The manuscript was discovered amongst the bishop's private papers. In parts it is very difficult to decipher, but what I have read has convinced me that Renton was quite right in refusing to open the vaults and that it is my bounden duty to continue his policy.'

'A manuscript which shocked you deeply, Mr Dean, and which you consider to be the work of Martin Railstone, though you admitted to knowing little about the man till recently.' However much he resisted it, an angry sneer was becoming apparent in Marne's voice. 'May I ask why you will not allow Mrs Wooderson, the acknowledged expert on the subject, to examine that manuscript?'

'For the simple reason that I have not finished reading it myself. I will tell you, however, that it is the portion of a diary, found in a drawer at Caswell Hall some weeks after Railstone was buried. He had clearly intended it to be placed with his other effects in the vaults and, unless the facsimiles shown in your book are inaccurate, madam, there is no doubt that the handwriting is Railstone's.' The Dean had been glaring at Marne, but he now transferred his anger to Mrs Wooderson.

'In that diary Martin Railstone admits to every sin, crime and abomination which your society have attempted to gloss over. The man was exactly as contemporary accounts describe him; a murderer, a sexual pervert and a blasphemer. Only senile dementia or a death-bed repentance could have prompted him to make that meaningless will with a clause that could never be fulfilled. For most of his life he was a monster and I, for one, shall feel extreme relief to know that his body and his works are buried beneath that reservoir.' Norseman glanced contemptuously at the books before him. 'I am afraid it will take much more than this evidence of supposed genius to persuade me otherwise.'

'But an interesting monster, Dr Norseman; an evil-doer of genius. Even though you do not appreciate Railstone's verse or his paintings, surely you must grant him that?' Erich Beck, Professor of Bacteriology at Lünefeld University, was a small untidy man in his late fifties. He had an expression which was both mild and slightly sinister and made one think of a forest gnome waiting to ensnare the lost traveller in one of the Grimms' grimmer fairy tales.

'I am not a member of the Caswellite Society, sir, but I have been interested in the details of Martin Railstone's life for a long time. As a scientist and a medical historian, I feel that . . .'

'I am aware of your professional qualifications, von Beck.' The Dean gave an angry snort. 'May I also say that I was stationed in Germany at the time of your trial and I heard the verdict with astonishment.'

Surely that was going a bit far, even for Norseman? John Wilde
looked up and waited for the German's rejoinder. During the war,
the Nazis had set up a medical research centre at Marienfeld concentration camp, and experiments had been carried out on living
human subjects. Beck was said to have visited the camp frequently
and in 1945 he had been arrested and brought before the Allied tribunal. But the evidence against him was so slight and inconclusive
that the judges had acquitted him without even retiring.

'You are naturally entitled to your opinions, sir.' No retort
came, only a polite bow and the flicker of sad eyes behind Beck's
glasses. 'But would you be kind enough to omit the *von* from my
name, Dr Norseman? Being an East German citizen, I am naturally bound to deplore the honorific.' He spoke very slowly and
his careful search for the correct English syntax made him sound
pedantic and stilted, but certainly not comic, however. Erich Beck
was a pigmy beside the Dean and a pauper compared with Marne.
But, as he watched his small humble face, John Wilde fancied that
he might be stronger than either of them.

'May I try and explain my position, ladies and gentlemen? Many
people, Mrs Wooderson and Lord Marne, for example, consider
Railstone to have been a very great writer and artist who became
insane towards the end of his life; not an uncommon occurrence
with men of genius.' Beck gave the merest hint of a smile.

'They believe that insanity caused him to draw up the will and
bury his works with him. They wish to open the tomb in the hope
that it will contain priceless examples of art and letters. I consider
that they may be right, though I have little appreciation of such
things. But may I ask you a question, Mrs Wooderson?

'Most critics agree that all Railstone's early work was trivial and
without value. At what date would you say his genius started to
flower, madam?'

'There is no doubt about that, Professor,' Marjorie Wooderson
replied in the clipped accents of Home Counties suburbia. She had
a thin haughty face and an expression which implied she had never
once been wrong in all her forty-odd years.

'Sir Martin displayed no great talent till *Sonnets to Martha* were
offered for publication in the February of 1750 and the first series

of "Dream Landscapes" were exhibited during the following June. He stated that both works had been produced simultaneously and in a period of under eighteen months.'

'Thank you, madam. And the book which interests me, *The Sceptical Philosopher*, was published in 1752. Railstone was over sixty when his greatest known works were produced, in fact. Surely that is rather a late age to receive inspiration?' Beck stooped and lifted a briefcase from the floor.

'Certain other people, and I do not deride them, consider that Railstone was a seer and a clairvoyant who worked under some supernatural influences and wonder if he left a record of his experiences in the tomb. You yourself, Dr Norseman, used the term diabolic possession. Perhaps you are right. Perhaps that was the reason for Sir Martin's sudden burst of genius. I have had no experience of the occult myself, but for all I know, such things may exist. I merely hope to discover the truth, whatever it is.' The German opened his case and produced a slim book bound in faded blue cloth.

'During most of his life Martin Railstone was an ordinary country landowner typical of his age. He dabbled in painting, verse and popular science, but showed no particular ability. A commonplace man who quite suddenly, while in his sixties, demonstrated extraordinary talents in several different fields. For five years he kept on demonstrating those talents and then, for no apparent reason, concealed them, though we know he was hard at work up to the time of his death in 1770.

'If I may, I would like to read you a passage written by Railstone in the early seventeen fifties.' Beck opened the book at a marker and squinted short-sightedly at the print.

'The Ancients believed that the human body was entire to itself, an isolated temple of flesh, governed by humours and an immaterial soul that dwelt within its walls but was not a part of it. But I am persuaded that the truth is very different. My body is not an empty temple, but a teeming city filled with countless tiny inhabitants and it is by their activities that our health and our maladies are decided.

'Since I took courage and ate of the fruit of wisdom,
so much knowledge and power has been given to me. I
now know that eventually, as long as I continue to follow
my daemon, every truth which perplexes mankind will
be revealed.'

Erich Beck closed the book and took off his glasses. Without their
thick lenses his eyes no longer appeared mild, but very hard and
intelligent.

'Dr Norseman, that was written seventy-two years before the
birth of Pasteur and a hundred and sixty years before the publication of Lister's *Antiseptic Principle in the Practice of Surgery*. At a
time when men hardly suspected the presence of microorganisms
in the human system, Railstone appears to have recognized them
and studied their nature in some detail.

'But how could he have done so? Where could he have found the
equipment? What was this fruit of knowledge and the daemon he
mentions? What caused his sudden burst of mental activity? The
upsurge of physical appetites too? From contemporary accounts
we know that Railstone was a regular client of a London brothel
up to the age of eighty. If the information is to be found in the
tomb, it might be of enormous importance to medical research.'

'Professor Beck, I am quite aware that the man suffered from
satyriasis as well as other diseases. But unless your profession has
made no advances since the time of Pasteur and Lister, surely the
interest is purely academic?' The Dean flicked ash from the cigar
and glanced at his watch. 'By the way, though I congratulate you
on your English vocabulary, I must point out that *daemon* is merely
a pedantic way of saying demon. You have done much to confirm
my own views on Railstone, Professor.

'Well, I have listened to three of you very patiently, but what
about the others? When may we expect to hear the roar of the
press, Mr Wilde? Does the *Daily Globe* intend to take me to task
because I refuse to resurrect the works of this supposed genius?
If so, let me tell you that my shoulders are quite broad enough to
bear your diatribes.'

'I'm sure they are, sir.' John grinned briefly. Though he might have appeared half asleep, he hadn't missed a word, but he was still uncertain how much news value the story contained. The death of Bishop Renton and the scheme to flood the valley might be worked together, but the majority of the *Globe's* readers would have little interest in Railstone's literary and artistic creations. Perhaps the best treatment would be to take the Dean's view and hint at devil worship, ancient debaucheries and dark supernatural forces that had been locked away in the tomb and were best left alone.

'The *Globe* is a popular paper, as you know, and though we have featured one article on the Caswell vaults, I am doubtful if we could use another. Lord Marne asked me to be present at this meeting, but I am still entirely neutral.' He leaned back in the chair and closed his eyes again.

'Now what about you, young woman?' Norseman scowled at Mary Carlin's mini-skirt and produced a bark that, though meant to be friendly, had terrified generations of soldiery out of their wits. 'Do you consider Railstone to have been a saint and a seer and an all-round genius as great as Leonardo? But pull down your dress, girl. Marne and Beck and I are too old to appreciate a strip-tease and Mr Wilde has gone back to sleep.'

'It is not Railstone himself that I'm interested in, Mr Dean.' Mary was a tall, fair girl usually jolly and self-possessed and she could look almost beautiful when she smiled. She was not smiling now. Norseman's reference to her skirt had made her even more flustered than when she had first come into the room and that was saying a good deal. She had a theory that fascinated her and a lot of work had gone into it. But her facts were so few, the clues so shadowy, that she dreaded voicing them to this obviously critical audience.

'My concern is with something much older than the story of Sir Martin, but which may have been lodged in the vaults beside his body.' Mary saw Beck replace his glasses and give her a long hard stare, and once again she regretted having asked to attend the meeting.

'You all know the inscription that is carved on the slab above Railstone's tomb. "A Red King Found Me" and so on. It is considered that three of the characters referred to are William Rufus, Stephen and Abbot Vulfrum, while the fourth is obviously Railstone himself. But who is the "Me" that keeps recurring?'

'Ah, we are going to hear about the Silver Orb.' Mrs Wooderson raised two prominent eyebrows. 'The relic of an unidentified saint which Rufus and Stephen are supposed to have had in their possession. There certainly is a local tradition that some such object found its way to Caswell Hall, but I imagined my book had established that the theory is quite untenable.

'But I mustn't interrupt a history don, must I?' Marjorie Wooderson was expert at making an apology sound far worse than the original insult. 'Please forgive me and proceed with your lecture, Miss Carlin.'

'Thank you.' Mary was cheered to see John Wilde open his eyes and give her a smile and a cynical wink. 'There is much more than legend and tradition to suggest that a relic of some sort existed, Mr Dean. To start with, a passage in the Bayard Chronicle substantiates that Rufus possessed an object so holy that he, an open mocker of Christianity, regarded it with extreme awe and terror.

'A thirteenth-century Welsh ballad then suggests that the thing consisted of two separate entities and that they fell into the hands of the usurper, Stephen.' John Wilde smiled again, Erich Beck was still staring fixedly at her, but the rest of her audience appeared bored and indifferent, and Mary hurried on, knowing that she was speaking dogmatically and blushing with embarrassment.

'But the most important reference is found in the records of Alfrastoun Castle. This clearly states that when Stephen was dying at Dover, he gave one of his knights, Roger de Senlis, "two most holy things" with instructions that they be placed beside the body of the "only good and wise man I ever knew". Shortly after Stephen's death, we find de Senlis at the court of Henry II, so it is problematic whether he carried out his orders in person. But I do think it likely that Stephen was referring to his friend, Abbot Vulfrum, who died six months before him. As you know, Vulfrum is buried here in Lanchester.'

'Naturally we know that, and what are you driving at, Miss Carlin?' Norseman had left the table and was standing by a window, watching the rooks circle the cathedral towers just as the bishop had done before the car crushed his body. 'Are we on the same subject, or do you want me to dig up the old abbot as well as Railstone?'

'No, sir, and I will try to explain if you will only give me a chance.' To hide her embarrassment and growing anger Mary studied the decor of the Dean's sitting-room, which varied from the bloodthirsty to the sentimental. Trophies of the chase were displayed on one wall, while another supported a collection of archaic weapons, all looking dangerously sharp. But between the windows hung *Bubbles*, flanked by *The Light of the World* and *The Shepherd's Last Mourner*, Edwin Landseer's neglected study of a gaunt, black-and-white collie stretched out upon his master's humble grave.

'In 1747, a slab at the side of Vulfrum's tomb was found to have been dislodged and clumsily replaced and, many years later, a man awaiting execution for robbery confessed that he was responsible. His story was that he had been approached by a gentleman in a London tavern who paid him five sovereigns to break into the tomb where he would find two metal objects. He was told to remove one of these and bring it to the tavern, but disturb nothing else. He never knew the name of his employer, but described him as being small and stout and with vividly red hair.' Mrs Wooderson yawned openly, Marne's fingers tapped on the table as if in irritation, and Mary raised her voice.

'Dr Norseman, I realize that there is not a great deal of evidence to go on. But, if one considers the inscription Railstone put over the slab, isn't it possible that those vaults may contain a relic once venerated by two Norman kings?'

'An extremely dubious possibility in my opinion, Miss Carlin.' The Dean had grown weary of the rooks and turned to face the table, stubbing out the cigar as he did so. 'In any case I have little faith in the authenticity of most religious relics. Scotland could not have produced enough timber to supply the fragments of the True Cross which are knocking about.

'Ladies and gentlemen, I have listened to you for a long time and not one of your arguments has persuaded me to change my mind. Railstone may have been a man of genius, as you say, Mrs Wooderson, but his verse and paintings mean very little to me. "To bring my second birth," indeed.' He snorted as Old Tom, the cathedral clock, began to strike the hour, and glanced meaningfully at his watch again.

'I am certain, however, that the man was both insane and extremely evil, and that no good would come of disturbing his remains. Whatever motives prompted him to make that eccentric will, the legal aspect remains quite clear. The diocese controls the Railstone trust and, as long as I remain in charge here, those vaults will remain sealed. Even if it means burying Miss Carlin's nebulous relic under a hundred feet of water.' The last note of the clock had boomed out across the precincts and Norseman moved to the door. He was just about to open it for his visitors when another dig at their expense occurred to him.

'But I am a reasonable man, so let me make a suggestion before you leave. Why not try to force my hand legally, Lord Marne? Devote your energies to locating the beneficiary mentioned in the will. Produce this female descendant bearing a close resemblance to Martin Railstone and persuade her to claim her legal rights. That's the only way you'll make me resurrect Little Boy Blue.' Norseman chuckled and then swung round angrily. Beyond the door came a woman's shouts and the sound of stumbling footsteps.

'What on earth is going on?' He pulled open the door, and George Banks came staggering into the room. His eyes were glazed, his face and clothing covered with grime, and from his left hand blood dribbled on to the carpet.

'Who are you, sir? How dare you come bursting in here? Is he drunk, Mrs Clarkson?'

'Either that or ill, sir.' Norseman's housekeeper had followed Banks into the room. 'I found him in the porch leaning against the bell push. He kept asking for you and when I said you were engaged he started to rave and carry on, like. Then he heard your voice and pushed his way past me.'

'Ill? Yes, I think you're right.' George stood swaying in front of him and Norseman's voice was suddenly kind as he looked at his face, dead white beneath the grime, and the blood which was not so much dribbling now as spurting from the cut in his hand. 'A motor accident, perhaps. Go and telephone the doctor, Mrs Clarkson.'

'What has happened to you, George? What are you doing here?' Marne helped the Dean to lower him into a chair. 'Tell me what on earth has been going on.'

'I came to speak to him . . . to the Dean, of course.' George spoke in gasps, his voice strong one instant, faltering the next, and there was a nervous tic at the corner of his mouth.

'You were right, sir. You and the bishops have been the only people to realize the danger.' He glanced at Marne and then, with what was obviously an enormous effort, reached out and clutched Norseman's sleeve.

'Don't let them open the tomb, Mr Dean. Fill in the entrance I made and then flood the whole accursed valley.' A second stream of blood appeared at his mouth and his lips crawled like scarlet worms.

'I have been down there. Right down into the vaults, and I heard it. Just before the wall fell and crushed me, I heard it clearly. Something laughing . . . something still alive after two hundred years.'

'Please stand aside. I am a doctor.' Erich Beck pushed between Marne and Norseman and knelt at George's side, feeling his pulse and frowning as he tied a handkerchief around the cut in his hand. 'Soon you will sleep, but first try to tell me everything that happened to you. Trust me, my friend, and try to remember exactly what you experienced in the vault?'

'A man's voice laughed at me. I touched something that was warm . . . it felt like human hair. Your book lied, Marjorie. Railstone was not insane when he made that will.' The red lips crawled on and the glazed eyes flickered from one face to another.

'Let them bury the valley, Lord Marne. Forget Martin Railstone, because he really was possessed and he knew that his body would not die. Either that or . . . or . . .' For a full ten seconds the word was repeated.

'Or he has a guardian.' The eyes closed, the head slumped forward and no more blood soaked through Beck's handkerchief. As

Gladys Thornton would have remarked, George Banks was as 'dead as a dodo'.

Four

'You still won't tell me what you think the actual nature of the relic might be?' John Wilde took a long swig of bitter beer. Almost two days had passed since Banks had died, and he and Mary Carlin were sitting in the saloon bar of a Lanchester public house. 'Coupled with the Dean's sinister diary, it might make quite a story.'

'I'm sure it would, but all I've got is a suspicion which I'm keeping to myself. There is no proper evidence at all, and if I told you what I suspect, your readers would think I'm as mad as everybody else connected with the vaults appears to be. Thanks.' She accepted a cigarette and leaned forward for him to light it.

'On the contrary, a treasure hunt is just the kind of thing my readers would enjoy, and I thought some of your evidence for the object's existence sounded pretty impressive – the story of the grave robber in particular.' John glanced at a copy of the *Globe* spread out on the table. Its headline demanded to know IS THERE A GUARDIAN OF THE TOMB? and his own name was prominently displayed beneath it.

'Are the others mad, if it comes to that? If the diary contains some really hot stuff, I can sympathize with Norseman's feelings, though I don't share them. The rank and file of the Caswellites are a mixed-up bunch, of course. The town was crawling with them earlier on, all rallying round to witness the Dean's ceremony this afternoon. One man told me that Railstone had been in contact with the gods of Ancient Egypt. A woman considered that he was a reincarnation of Merlin. Another chap said he had drunk the elixir of life and that his body will have remained uncorrupted in the vaults and he is merely sleeping and waiting to be awakened like Arthur or Barbarossa.' John nibbled at a cheese sandwich and downed it with whisky and another beer chaser. He was the kind of man who lived largely on snacks and felt most at home in bars and hotels, ships' saloons and airport lounges.

'The top people are sane enough, though; Marne, Mother Wooderson and Beck. After all, if Railstone did leave some important work down there, surely it's reasonable to want to recover it. And, as Beck said, it does seem strange that he should burst into activity so late in life. Talking of Beck, where is the damned fellow? He should be here by now.' John looked at the bar clock. At three o'clock sharp the Dean intended to reseal the vault with some ceremony. Mary had offered to drive him and Beck to Caswell Hall, and time was getting on.

'I can tell you one thing, Mary. Marne is not the kind of man to give up easily, and you may still have a chance to look for your relic. Old Norseman may spatter holy water and read the riot act to his heart's content, but Lord Marne, K.C.M.G., O.B.E., and all the rest of it is a very tough customer and he'll fight him to the last ditch.'

'He's tough all right. I imagined Marne and Banks were friends, but he showed no emotion at all when Banks died.' Mary frowned as John finished his whisky, chased it with more beer, and beckoned to the waiter to bring him another. He looked fit enough, but obviously drank far too much and probably never ate a decent meal unless forced to entertain in the way of business.

'Beck puzzles me though, John. He may be interested in Railstone, but to come all the way from Germany is a bit drastic. And why did he go to the coroner and ask for an autopsy on Banks? We know exactly what happened. Banks's own doctor said that he was mentally disturbed, possibly schizophrenic, and might easily have imagined unreal phenomena. The laughter he said he heard must have been the rumble of the brickwork which injured him as he left the vault. Beck himself agreed that one of his vertebro-sternal ribs had been driven into a lung causing the haemorrhage which finally killed him.' Mary picked up the newspaper and shook her head.

'First Beck makes a mystery of Banks's death and then you produce this. "The Guardian of the Tomb", indeed. Hints of supernatural forces at work and some kind of Glamis horror which has been walled up with Railstone's body since the eighteenth century. How can you write such tosh, John?'

'Because it's the kind of tosh my readers enjoy, Mary.' John paid the waiter and toyed with his fresh whisky. 'And you're a fine one to talk, my dear. After all isn't my "guardian", supernatural or mortal, just as credible as your medieval relic?

'Seriously though, there was something a bit uncanny about the way Banks died, and Beck is an internationally respected scientist. The actual cause of death was an internal haemorrhage caused by the broken rib, but did you notice how violently the blood spurted from his hand and mouth just before he died? Everything was so rapid, too. Norseman's housekeeper said that he pushed past her with a good deal of strength, but a few minutes later he just sort of withered. But here comes the Herr Doktor himself to tell us of his findings.'

Through the window Beck's slight figure was hurrying across the street and they finished their drinks and stood up. As they stepped on to the pavement, John nodded towards a poster displayed on a passing delivery van. It advertised a product named 'Rover's Romp' and showed a gentleman fast asleep in a deck chair, while a few yards away from him a large and jovial Alsatian bounded across a suburban garden obviously in pursuit of prey or a bitch on heat. 'That is one of Marne's most profitable commodities and he's very proud of it. Whenever he makes an after-dinner speech he boasts that he earns a fortune out of canine aphrodisiacs. Proves what a cynical blighter the man is.

'Well, Professor, can you tell us what the post mortem showed?' Mary had taken the wheel with Beck sitting beside her and John leaned forward over the seat. 'Was there a secondary cause of death, as you thought?'

'There was, but it may be a perfectly natural one, Mr Wilde.' Beck looked tired and dispirited and he fiddled with an old, blackened pipe as if to steady his nerves. 'The rapidity of the internal and external bleeding still strikes me as being curious. Sir Gordon Lampton, the county pathologist, on the other hand, has an explanation for this.

'There is no doubt that the poor fellow died of a haemorrhage but, by itself, the injury to the lung would not have killed him. Do you mind if I smoke, Miss Carlin? Thank you.' In silence and with agonizing slowness, Beck unrolled a pouch and started to fill the pipe. His slim fingers worked as precisely as a surgeon's and as John and Mary waited they both considered his past.

Beck had been acquitted by the tribunal in 'forty-five because there was no definite evidence that he had been anywhere near the Marienfeld camp, let alone been a member of its staff. But were the charges true, they wondered? Had those hands, now innocently filling a pipe, once prepared a culture of plague or typhus and injected it into a human body? Certainly some very horrible experiments had taken place at Marienfeld, and Mary winced at the thought that the tribunal might have been wrong, while John, who had been a newspaper man for half of his thirty-six years, felt a slight spasm of distaste at sharing the car with him.

'Sir Gordon Lampton believes that Banks must have suffered from Rheinfelder's syndrome – a condition of the autonomic nervous system which speeds up the action of the heart unduly if the subject is under mental stress.' Beck had lit the pipe at last and he pulled gently at it as he talked.

'Sir Gordon may well be right. Both ventricles showed signs of the intense stretching which is characteristic of the complaint. Also, the abnormal heart action produced by the syndrome could account for the rapidity of the bleeding and the failure of the external wound to congeal. Without that heart action, Banks might still be alive, though a bad . . . bad . . . what is the word? Versicherungsrisiko? Insurance risk, of course. Thank you, Mr Wilde. My mother was English, we had an English governess, but I am sadly out of practice.'

'Then there is no real mystery, Professor?' John had pulled out his shorthand pad but he laid it down. 'George Banks died because the haemorrhage was aggravated by this nervous condition, Rheinfelder's disease?'

'Provided he suffered from Rheinfelder's syndrome. On my request Sir Gordon telephoned the man's own medical adviser in London, a Dr Singh. Singh told him that he had given Banks a thorough check three months ago and that there was nothing wrong with his heart.'

'Surely that's unlikely.' They were out of the town now and

Mary frowned as she accelerated down the open road leading towards the Cass Valley. 'I thought the condition was slow and progressive. Could the doctor have been mistaken?'

'You share Lampton's views, Miss Carlin.' Beck watched the rolling landscape spread out before them and some of the tiredness they had noticed earlier had left his face. 'Sir Gordon has a poor opinion of foreigners in general and of Indians in particular. However, he did agree to send certain specimens to London for chemical analysis and we will just have to wait for the report.'

'Chemical analysis?' John's pencil was busily at work and he raised his eyebrows. 'Are you suggesting that Banks died because some drug caused his abnormal heart condition?'

'I am suggesting nothing, Mr Wilde. I am merely puzzled. Sir Gordon could be quite correct in his diagnosis, and Banks may have suffered from Rheinfelder's syndrome. All the same, its symptoms are easily detected in a living subject and I should have thought any second-year student would have spotted them.' He paused as Mary slowed down to pass a convoy of four heavy lorries. They were all loaded with earth-moving equipment and obviously on their way to the site of the dam.

'As you are, of course, aware, there are many substances which increase the action of the heart. Strychnine comes to mind at once, but we would have detected its presence without difficulty. On the other hand there are certain anti-histamine preparations which dilate the capillaries and are less easy to isolate. If Banks had taken an enormous overdose of such a drug, it might have remained in his system for a long time and produced the abnormal blood pressure which killed him.'

'Would it also have produced mental excitement, Professor? We know that Banks was mentally unstable, but he was not insane. Do you think he might have been under the influence of drugs when he decided to break into the vault? If so, that would account for his delusions about hearing the laughter and touching something warm.'

The editorial conference had been sceptical when John proposed that Renton's death and the announcement of the reservoir scheme made Caswell Hall a lead story, and the conference had been wrong. For two days his suggestions that dark forces could be lurking in the vaults had appeared on the front page and now another possible angle to the story had occurred to him. The bishop had been killed by a hit-and-run driver, and Banks because of a heart condition which might possibly have been caused by chemical action. The two men were in opposite camps, but they were both obsessed with the history of Martin Railstone. Could somebody have paid the driver of the car? Had somebody persuaded Banks to break into the vaults? If so, what other preparations besides Rover's Romp might have been produced in the laboratory of Lord Marne?

'Provided an extremely large dose had been administered, there would certainly be some mental alteration, Mr Wilde. But personally I do not believe traces of any such drug will be found. What I suspect is something quite different.' Beck shook his head as the road topped a rise and started to wind down into the valley.

'Why talk about it, though? Perhaps Sir Gordon's diagnosis is correct and Banks did suffer from the syndrome. In any case we must wait for the analyst's report. Is that the house over there?'

Caswell Hall was in sight and Mary felt Beck stiffen at her side. 'For more than five years I have wished to come here, but the East German People's Republic is a hard mistress and only last week was I given permission to take a leave in England. And now I am too late, and the truth will never be known. Because of a bigot like Norseman, a superstitious throwback to the Middle Ages who believes in diabolic possession and such mumbo-jumbo, the darkness must continue.' At the end of the valley the earth had been stripped to show a scar of white rock and they could see trucks and bulldozers moving across it. 'Must there always be such men to keep us from the truth?'

'The truth about Martin Railstone, Professor?' Mary was struck by the sudden change in Beck's tone. Until a moment ago he had been talking quietly, but as the foundations of the dam came into view his voice had become strident and angry.

'Yes, Miss Carlin. I wanted to know what were the daemon and the fruit of knowledge he wrote about. Why should such a commonplace man suddenly develop a great varied burst of creative energy so late in life: art, poetry and scientific inquiry? Could there have been a physiological change, perhaps? An alteration in the glandular structure? Could the relic you talked about have had some connection with that late development of genius?' Beck spoke with the pipe clenched tightly between his teeth and his voice was still angry.

'Years ago I witnessed a very similar phenomenon, though it happened to a young child. From the day I started to study the life of Martin Railstone I asked myself if his was a parallel case. But why discuss it? Soon the Dean will carry out his own Burning of the Books and the evidence will be buried.'

'What happened to the child, Professor?' Once again Mary was struck by the savagery in his voice and she remembered how reasonably he had put his case to Norseman; a scholar demanding information in the interests of research.

'He died, Miss Carlin, and there is no point in talking about him.' Beck lowered the window to knock out his pipe and Mary glanced at his profile, seeing the skin taut against the cheekbone and anger in his eye. The Nazi phrase 'Burning of the Books' made her think of his trial again, and she tried to imagine Beck standing in the dock at Nuremberg; younger, more erect, not so bald, but the same man. As she drove through the gates of the hall and the wheels crunched on gravel she seemed to hear the voices of the judges acquitting him. 'Not guilty . . . insufficient evidence . . . not guilty.' Then, for no reason at all, her own voice shouting 'Guilty . . . guilty as Hell.'

'The lair of the Guardian.' John's cynical chuckle interrupted her thoughts. 'It looks pleasant enough today, but I'd like to see it in really bad weather.' The house lay straight before them, friendly and welcoming under a clear sky, and to the left the waters of the lake sparkled in the sunlight. 'The Dean has gathered quite a good audience for his performance.'

The car park had been half empty on the day that Banks tunnelled to his death, but now it was almost full, and Mary had some difficulty in finding a vacant space. The time was practically three when they got out of the car and started to walk round towards the back of the house.

'The world and his wife have turned up.' John produced a camera and took several shots of the scene before them. The crowd was largely composed of local people and ordinary tourists with a few reporters dotted amongst them, but a phalanx of bearded and sandalled figures showed that the Caswellites were there in force. A pile of shattered brickwork was visible beyond the disused moat and some fifty yards in front of the moat stood a group of clergymen, with Norseman towering in their midst, very gay in the robes of a Doctor of Divinity. To the right of the clergy was stationed a large yellow concrete tanker with its driver in position at the controls.

'Good afternoon to you all.' Lord Marne had stepped out from the edge of the crowd and came smiling towards them. 'What a lovely day for it and we are to have the full treatment, I understand. A legal harangue, a religious ceremony and a demonstration of civil engineering techniques.'

'You don't seem concerned, Lord Marne.' Mary had to raise her voice against a Salvation Army band which was rendering *Onward Christian Soldiers* with more vigour than harmony. She suddenly felt as much frustration as Beck had shown in the car. Beyond that heap of broken brickwork might lie an object that two kings had venerated, and soon the reservoir would bury it for ever. It was two years since Mary had started to take an interest in the legend, and at first she had regarded it with scepticism. But as, one after the other, disjointed scraps of information began to fit together: local tradition, parish records and monastery rolls, and above all the Alfrastoun and Bayard accounts, the quest for the relic had grown into a personal challenge. She had not dared to tell her closest friends what she considered the thing to be, but if her guess was right, that tomb might contain one of the greatest treasures in Christendom.

'The valley may be under water before a new bishop is even enthroned. Our best hope was to persuade the Dean to change his mind, and he won't do that after today.'

'Quite correct, Miss Carlin. I imagine that is one of the reasons for this monkey show – to demonstrate that he cannot go back on his word.' Marne was watching the scene with quiet amusement. The Salvationists had started their last chorus and the clergy were forming two lines with Norseman standing between them on his own. 'Yes, the Dean is proving as stubborn an obstacle as the lamented bishop. Perhaps kindly fortune will provide us with another hit-and-run driver.

'However, don't despair, my dear. There is ample time at our disposal. Was it General de Gaulle who said "We have lost a battle, not a war"? I am a true example of the self-made man, Miss Carlin. I started life in a slum and I have had to fight for everything I wanted. Now I want to know what those vaults contain. Believe me when I tell you that I shall go on fighting and that there are a few cards up my sleeve.'

'The fools. The superstitious, ignorant fools.' Beck was watching the Dean and his party, who were moving towards the house; their robes proudly swinging, thuribles clanking and incense rising in the still air. 'Why does that animal meddle in matters he can never hope to understand? Why are there always such men to stand in the way of knowledge and scientific inquiry?'

'An animal indeed, Professor, but what a noble one.' Marne chuckled as the clergy reached the edge of the moat and the Dean turned and stood silently facing the crowd as if challenging interruptions. 'You don't usually find 'em as large as that in captivity. Look at the great shoulders on him and the way he holds himself. Look at the faith in the feller's eyes. Believe me, he's going to need every scrap of that faith before I've done with him.'

'My friends . . . I hope I may call you my friends.' Norseman's voice came rolling across the crowd. 'Two days ago a man came to this place and performed an insane and criminal action which led to his death.' A right arm, robed in scarlet and black, pointed to the pile of rubble across the moat.

'You will all have read accounts of this in the press and there is no need for me to remind you of the harrowing details. I have merely come here today to perform three duties, and the first is to issue a warning which I hope will be clearly understood.'

Norseman spoke with obvious relish and the warning could hardly have failed to be understood. In future no members of the public would be admitted to the grounds except under strict supervision, and he pointed out the legal penalties for housebreaking and the certainty of capture should anybody be foolhardy enough to make a second attempt on the vaults. Additional barbed wire and an electrical warning system had already been installed. 'Prot-Corps' guards would be on duty day and night. Last, but certainly not least, savage dogs would be at hand to deal with interlopers. John was certain that the diocese would never stand such expense and most of the threats were idle boasts. But the Dean made the place sound as impregnable as a fortress, and a few cries of 'shame' and 'disgrace' were easily quelled by the power of his lungs.

'Having delivered these civil warnings, I will now carry out my second duty.' A slight breeze had started to blow in from the sea and Norseman's robes flowed around him like a martial cloak.

'Beneath this building is buried the body of a bad man; a self-confessed murderer, a debauchee, a man who meddled with things of the darkness.

'Madam, there is no need to tell me your name.' A woman had shouted 'liar' and he paused and crushed her with a long contemptuous glare.

'Whatever irresponsible people may tell you, my friends, there is quite definite evidence that Martin Railstone was all of these things. However, since, towards the end of his life, he handed over his body and possessions into the safe-keeping of the Church, there is also some evidence to suggest that he may have repented of his evil ways. It is therefore my intention to bless this building in the hope that I will give peace to any troubled spirit that lurks within its walls.' He bowed to the right and left, and was answered by a clank of thuribles.

'Oh creature, I adjure thee by the living God, by the holy God . . .' The Dean had bent his head in prayer and two of his assistants had stepped down into the moat and were spattering the wall with holy water.

'Root out and expel the enemy, O Lord . . . Let not the spirit of pestilence abide herein . . . May this place be free from all uncleanness . . . Let the darkness be replaced by the light of Thy countenance . . .' If Norseman had lacked a single grain of faith it would have been comic, but before the prayers came to an end, both John and Mary felt slightly awed by the complete conviction in his voice.

'We have not quite finished, my friends. I have sealed these vaults with the power of God, our Father, and now they will be closed by Man, His servant.' He bowed to the driver of the tanker and its engine burst into a pulsing bellowing roar that seemed to shake the whole valley. The operation had obviously been rehearsed and, as Norseman and his entourage stepped aside the big crawler lumbered into the ditch, the driver pulled a lever, and a stream of liquid concrete spewed over the rubble and the breach in the wall. Water, the Word, and quick-setting cement had obliterated George Banks's labours, and the business was concluded.

'Ah, there you are, Lord Marne. I am delighted you were able to attend our little ceremony.' The Dean came striding through the crowd. 'Everything went very well, I think, and it was a nice touch getting the reservoir contractors to lend that juggernaut as a final gesture; a symbol of the deluge to come. By the way, I have a piece of news for you. It is now quite certain that the bishopric will be offered to David Sommerlees of Grantham. But he's abroad on a lecture tour, and can't possibly be enthroned for several months. Not before those chaps have finished their work and the reservoir is an accomplished fact.' He nodded at the tanker snorting away down the drive.

'Your only hope is to bring legal pressure on me, Lord Marne.' Norseman produced a cigar case from the depths of his robe and his eyes twinkled in preparation for the worn joke. 'Find that female mentioned in the will and on the inscription above the slab. "Dove è la Donna che Mi può dare la Vita." "She who can deliver me," as your friend, Mrs Wooderson, so loosely translated the jingle.'

'Quite so, and please allow me.' Marne smiled back and held out a cigarette lighter. 'What a very strange coincidence you should remind me of that, today of all days.' His smile widened as he lit Norseman's cigar.

'You see, Mr Dean, I rather think that I may have found her.'

Five

THE next morning, a million readers of the *Daily Globe* opened their mid-week colour supplement and the Railstone controversy ceased to be a wrangle between two small groups of people and became a national issue, because John Wilde had gone to town.

The cover bore the title 'Monster or Saint', and displayed two contemporary portraits of Martin Railstone. One showed the bluish face smiling benevolently out from the canvas, while in the other he glowered like a tortured fiend beneath his shock of red hair.

John had repeated the 'Glamis Horror' and the 'Guardian of the Tomb' possibilities, and hinted at the enormous treasures that the vaults might contain. He had written an account of George Banks's death with much moving detail and finally given the comments of the main protagonists.

> Lord Marne, level-headed man of business, told me, 'Martin Railstone's works belong to mankind and mankind shall have them.'
>
> Mrs Marjorie Wooderson, scholar and best-selling romantic novelist, said, 'As I hope I made clear in my biography of Railstone, *A Light at Midnight*, Sir Martin was a tortured spirit, but the tales of his wickedness are pure invention. The vaults must be opened in the teeth of bigotry and reaction.'
>
> Professor Erich Beck, the internationally respected scientist . . . Miss Mary Carlin, one of the country's most promising young historians . . .

A Q.C. to clarify the legal aspects . . . a lunatic who believed Railstone had discovered the secret of perpetual motion . . . a poet and an art critic . . . the president of the Occult Inquiry League, who suggested that both *The Inner Darkness* and the 'Dream Landscapes' had been produced while Railstone was under some supernatural influence . . . a society hostess and a Cambridge don. All these people pressed that the vaults should be opened, but John had given the opposition the last word. Beneath a half-page photograph of Dr Norseman, whom he described as 'a former general officer of the British Army, a brave man, a dedicated man, a man deeply concerned with the problem of good and evil', lay the Dean's terse defiance: 'I can only repeat that I will not yield an inch.'

By the time they had finished the supplement, ninety-nine per cent of its readers were convinced. Whatever the Caswell vaults contained – works of genius or the ravings of a man who had died insane; information about the occult or some nameless physical horror; a medieval relic or merely bones and worthless scraps of paper – they wanted the tomb opened. Before the day was out several hundred letters were on their way to M.P.s and newspapers.

Not a bad piece of work at all, John thought as he turned the last glossy page. Feeling well pleased with himself, he poured out another cup of coffee and smiled at the clear sky through the office window. The summer had been hot and dry and most people considered the autumn would be the same. But already a United States satellite was informing its masters that most people were wrong and bad weather was on the way.

'Good morning, Peter.' The telephone had rung and John greeted the paper's medical correspondent. 'Did you manage to get that dope on Beck for me?' The German's bitter outburst in the car had persuaded him to take an interest in his career. Beck's concern with Railstone was clearly more personal than that of a normal scientific research worker or medical historian, and it seemed important to know what it was.

'Naturally I did, John. Erich Beck is a pretty big pot and his work is well known. I had most of the information in my head.' Dr Peter Franklin had an irritatingly superior manner and a cultivated lisp which he considered to show good breeding.

'Beck's most important research dealt with cell degeneration. He also published several papers on the action of micro-organisms on mental processes. You'd better take this down in writing, John, as some of it is pretty technical.'

Franklin was as good as his word, always using a specialized term where a general one would have sufficed, and John's mind reeled beneath a battering of Latin and Greek. But slowly a picture began to fit together.

Erich Beck's studies had followed two main lines of inquiry. The first was to discover why, when deprived of blood, the brain cells should decay so much sooner than those of the rest of the body. That inquiry had led him to stand in the dock at Nuremberg and John felt more than slightly sick as he realized what the man had been charged with.

'Even a layman knows about cerebral degeneration, old boy,' Franklin had lisped. 'Arrest the heart for a period of time, deprive the organism of fresh blood, then restart it, and what happens? The body recovers. Limbs, internal organs, muscles, they all become active again and no harm is done. But not the brain, because the cells have withered, degenerated. During his early days, Beck had attempted to discover the actual time-factors involved and that's what got him into trouble.'

'Yes, I know about that, Peter.' John had spent an hour going through the paper's old files. Beck had been concerned with cerebral degeneration, and experiments to establish its causes were known to have been carried out on human subjects at Marienfeld concentration camp. Beck was rumoured to have visited the camp several times during 1944 and six witnesses, three of them children, had been produced in the hope that they might recognize him. A very vain hope indeed. The experiments had turned each of those witnesses into an imbecile who would have had difficulty in recognizing its own face in a mirror.

But, as Franklin now explained, Beck's second line of inquiry appeared innocent enough: he was engaged on research as to why certain illnesses could also produce beneficial results. How, for instance, did Parkinson's disease tend to prolong life? Why did many consumptives and epileptics show abnormal creative and sexual powers, and sufferers from muscular dystrophy sometimes have a capacity for intense concentration?

'Thank you, Peter. You have been most helpful.' John replaced the telephone and took a sip of lukewarm coffee. As he did so, he pictured Beck's tense face in the car and remembered his exact words: ' . . . a great burst of creative energy so late in life. Could there have been a physiological change, perhaps? An alteration of the glandular structure?'

Beck clearly believed that that might have been the case, but what did he hope to discover after such a period of time? That Railstone had been afflicted by some physical illness which turned him almost overnight from potterer to genius? That he might have left records of his symptoms to identify the malady?

A dead child on an operating table returning to life when an electric shock was applied to stimulate the heart. Limbs moving, the pulse beating steadily, and the eyes opening. But behind the eyes death remained, because the brain had withered. Had Erich Beck once witnessed that? Did he also imagine that the vaults at Caswell Hall might contain material for further experiments? John forced the images aside, but they kept recurring, and towards noon another notion joined them. Was it possible that Beck was interested not in Railstone's papers, but in his body?

★　★　★

While John was listening to Peter Franklin, Mr Kingsley Virgil Isaacs was also on the telephone, answering an urgent query from Colonel Mortimer, managing director of Messrs Spender-Wade, the contractors for the Cass River Scheme.

Yes, Mr Isaacs had heard the long-range weather forecast only a few minutes ago. Yes, he realized that if the weather did deteriorate as badly as was predicted they might be in for trouble. However, there could be no question of postponing operations till the spring because Thornhanger New Town already needed the water. No, Mr Isaacs was not at all perturbed, because he knew Spender-Wade's reputation for overcoming difficulties. Had Colonel Mortimer heard that the Germans were well ahead of schedule and the concrete sections were already being loaded at Rotterdam? Yes, they would reach Southampton on the second of next month instead of the eighth as had been anticipated. The work would have to be speeded, that was all. More men and equipment must be brought to the site so that the main structure was in position before the weather broke. That was the key point of the design, of course. As Mr Isaacs had pointed out earlier, speed and simplicity had been his chief aims. Once the foundations were ready the sections could be fitted together and buttressed in no time at all.

But of course he realized that the original tenders could no longer apply and there would be considerable additional expense. Perhaps Colonel Mortimer would call him back when he'd prepared a fresh estimate. Though the Minister deplored squandering public money, the reservoir was a national necessity and Mr Isaacs was sure he would not worry about a further hundred thousand pounds or so, providing, of course, that the main structure was firmly braced before the end of the month.

Yes, that should be quite satisfactory. Mr Isaacs replaced the telephone feeling elated that Nature had decided to give his brain child a premature birth.

*   *   *

That morning, having finished a hearty breakfast of bacon, eggs, kidneys and sausages, Dr William Norseman resumed his studies of the Railstone diary. The ink was faded, many of the pages were torn and yellowed, but Railstone had had a remarkably firm hand for his age and the Dean was able to read, though with some difficulty.

> London, Nov. 15th 1761. Last night dined with my bookseller and publisher, Charles Peacock, a presumptuous man who keeps pressing for details of the work I am engaged upon. At times Peacock can be amusing company, but my refusals appeared to distress him and he drank beyond the bounds of temperance, forgetting both his manners and his normal principles. Before collapsing and being carried away by the cellar boys, he delivered a drunken diatribe against not only established religion, but the very existence of a supernatural world. If only Peacock knew what I know, if only my fellow men shared my

visions and I could enroll their help, the darkness would be lifted so much sooner.

Yes, my burden is very great, though I have been given the mental powers of a Newton and the back of a Hercules. While Peacock snored, I repaired to Martha Johnson's establishment in Vauxhall where I did enjoy no less than four of her drabs in as many hours.

In spite of his horror of the man, the Dean gave a low whistle of admiration. Railstone had been in his late seventies when the passage was written.

Caswell Hall, Nov. 21st. A sad return from London to find Kate three days dead and rotting in her bonds. In life she was a worthless vagrant and has proved as worthless a subject for my purpose. In future I must be more selective and seek only those with the exact physical requirements that have been given to me.

Nov. 22nd. Kate's body is disposed of and my boy, Tom, has made pure the laboratory with sulphur. But the stench of decomposition still persists in the house to add to my sense of frustration.

Norseman closed the book with a snap, bitterly regretting his excellent breakfast.

⋆   ⋆   ⋆

Also that morning, Lord Marne examined his trump card. He had returned to London after Norseman's ceremony and stood with his back to a window overlooking Regent's Park. On the opposite wall hung his most prized possession, one of the very few self-portraits of Martin Railstone in private hands. In it, the artist was shown leaning against a twisted pinnacle of rock which curled over his small body like a breaking wave. His face was in shadow and almost invisible against the slate-blue stone, while the background was composed of more rocks, all curiously formed, and a clump of stunted trees. The general effect of the picture was unearthly and dream-like, and this was heightened by two pale suns or moons placed in the upper corners of the canvas with rays intersecting above Railstone's vividly red hair.

'I want the absolute truth, Buller.' Marne frowned at the man who lay stretched out on a sofa to the right of the painting. 'Long ago, when I considered taking the law into my own hands, we decided that an impostor might be employed: a clever actress supported by the necessary physical qualifications and forged documents to convince a court that she was a member of the Railstone family and the heiress to the trust. For two years you have been looking for such an actress and only now, at the very last minute, you say that you have found her. I repeat that I want the truth. How good is our claimant? What chance is there that she will pass muster?'

'It's not a question of chance, sir. This is a certainty, as you will soon see for yourself.' Eton and Oxford had given Vincent Buller a beautifully modulated voice, but he could best be described as a grubby man. His jaw had a dark stubble, his teeth were yellow, his suit unpressed and his shoes unpolished, and at the moment he was engaged in picking his nose with a dirty thumb-nail.

'You know that I've always been extremely dubious about this claimant scheme, Lord Marne. Your very generous payments and your enthusiasm – may I say obsession – to open the tomb have urged me on, but, as a member of the College of Heralds and a barrister-at-law . . .'

'A disbarred barrister-at-law, Buller. A member of the college who was dismissed with ignominy.' Marne loathed the very sight and sound and musty smell of the man and would never have employed him if he could have found somebody else with his talents.

'But not disbarred because I didn't know my job, Lord Marne. Dismissed for malpractice, not incompetence.' If a rat could smile it would have looked very much like Vincent Buller. 'Shall we get down to business?'

He nodded towards a book and number of documents spread out on the table. 'The family tree will pass muster, I'm certain of that, and there's only one link in the chain which has the slightest weakness.' He pulled himself wearily out of the sofa and crossed to the table.

'Railstone's half-sister, Joan, Lady Reynolds, as she became by marriage after her brother's death, gave birth at the remarkably late age of forty-eight. The child, a boy named Adam, qualified as a physician and settled in Cumberland where he married a Miss Rachel Alison of Carlisle. Their union was also blessed with issue; two boys, the first of which died in infancy, and a daughter. I was unable to discover anything about the second boy, but we shall show a direct line from the daughter to a woman now living in London.' Buller's grimy hands fumbled through the documents.

'Here is the marriage certificate of Dr Adam Reynolds and Miss Alison. Here is a letter written to Reynolds by his mother. Here is a bill of sale executed on Reynolds's practice when he retired. Here is the gem of my collection.' He pushed the small volume, which was bound in badly rubbed calf, across the table to Marne.

'Yes, I thought that would interest you, sir. A first edition of *Sonnets to Martha* with the inscription "This book was inspired by the character of Martha Johnson, a brothel-owner. I send it to my sister with affection and the hope that she may one day learn to control her shrewish temper." Rather strange that Lady Reynolds should have kept such a gift. That was the weakness of the chain I mentioned.'

'It's good, Buller. Yes, I must congratulate you, because it's very, very good indeed.' Marne held a magnifying glass over the fly leaf. He had studied a great many Railstone manuscripts and the forgery appeared faultless. There would have to be a chemical test on the ink and paper of the other documents, of course, but Buller knew his job and that was the least of their worries.

'But what about the woman herself? That's the key point. Even with impeccable forgeries, she will have to do more than act. Before she can satisfy a court, she'll almost have to convince herself that she's a descendant of the Railstones. Time's running out, you know, and we must work fast.'

'I am aware of that, but there is no need to worry.' Buller produced a photograph. 'Here is our claimant, sir. Her name is Miss Nancy Leame, and she resides in Fulham.'

The photograph was in colour and showed a youngish woman standing before the camera. The woman was very stout, rather shabbily dressed and her vividly red hair was drawn far back from her broad forehead. Though the picture had been carefully posed, the smile in her mouth and eyes hinted at extreme nervousness.

'I just don't understand.' Marne felt waves of disappointment as he studied the heavy features and the sagging body. 'You bloody fool, Buller. This woman may have the physical characteristics mentioned in the will, but I don't believe she could act. She looks too nervous to hold her own in a game of charades.'

'I'm not a fool, sir; only a crook.' Buller gave a throaty chuckle. 'I was kicked out of the college because a client boasted about his forged family tree, and disbarred because my partner let me down.

'You're right about Miss Leame, of course. Poor Nancy is a most disturbed creature; been in and out of mental homes since she was a young girl: very nervous indeed and it would take her months to learn the part. All the same, with these documents British justice will give us the verdict. Nothing is going to go wrong and the sooner we allow the gentlemen of the press to interview our claimant the better.' He chuckled again and slapped a copy of the *Globe* stuffed in a pocket of his baggy jacket.

'Don't you understand what I'm telling you? Can't you see the joke? For almost two years you've been paying me to find a talented actress to break the Railstone trust and now we don't need one.' Buller's chuckles became great belches of mirth and Marne drew back before a blast of stale whisky and gingivitis that was quite undiminished by 'Fearless', one of his own chemical products, designed to defeat the breathalyser test and unofficially known as the 'Motorist's Friend'.

'She can't act and she won't have to act.' Buller wiped his streaming eyes. 'For once in a while I'm going to win a case honestly, because those documents are not forgeries. Every damn one of them is genuine and Nancy Leame is the real thing.'

*   *   *

Late that afternoon the Dean returned to the diary. After the record of Kate's end and burial, a large section of the book was missing and the next entry was dated three years later.

Caswell Hall, Jan. 3rd, 1764. The sudden loss of my dear friend and faithful retainer, Charles Rector, is a heavy burden to bear. Though an uneducated peasant and a convicted felon whom I saved from the gallows by bribery, Rector possessed more intelligence, loyalty and spiritual perception than most clerics of his title. He will be deeply missed by a grateful master.

January 12th. Rector's peaceful passing, coupled with the unseemly end of the little Cheapside whore who died denying me those pleasures which were mine by right of purchase, persuades me that my earlier anxieties may not be groundless. So that I may cause no harm to my fellow creatures I have taken the precaution of wearing gloves and ordered my few remaining attendants to do the same when they are near me. Whether this touch of death exists or not, I must be careful till I know the truth.

Jan. 24th. Am invited to dine with General Lockie of Thorne. A man who has often bored me with his Iberian travels and enthusiasm for the Spanish bullfight; which recreation sounds very tame when compared to our good old English sport of bull-baiting. On this occasion, I intend to forego my usual precautions and shake my host warmly with the bare hand.

Norseman grunted with relief. Touch of death indeed! Were his anxieties groundless? Had Railstone invented the abominations he described? Was he a harmless lunatic unable to distinguish fact from fantasy? He turned the page and his eyebrows came up in a bar beneath his forehead.

Feb. 5th. Let us hope that Hell is a warmer and more comfortable establishment than Thorne Castle. This afternoon I was informed that Angus Lockie had died of a sudden seizure.

Six

IT was going to be a savage autumn, there was no doubt about that. From all over the world, instruments on ships and mountains and high buildings confirmed the satellite's forecast. When the weather broke it would break dramatically. But, for a while, the long hot summer continued.

In the Cass Valley, Spender-Wade's men cursed the summer. The heat settled in the pocket of the valley, attracting swarms of midges and flying ants which made life intolerable. But, though they grumbled, they were on piece work; additional equipment had been brought in from other sites, they had been promised a bonus for early completion, and they worked. Day and night the bulldozers scraped away the topsoil to reveal the firm Portland stone, the valley echoed with the sound of drills cutting slots to contain piers and buttresses, and concrete mixers spewed out the foundations. Before the month was out Mr Isaacs' wildest hopes were fulfilled and the first prefabricated section had been hoisted into position, standing before Caswell Hall like the vanguard of an advancing army. When the rains came there would be a girdle of steel and concrete to contain them.

In London, Sir Gordon Lampton was also feeling the heat and he mopped his elegant forehead as he frowned over a report from the research laboratory to which he had sent specimens taken from the body of George Banks. Its author stated that he was unable to confirm or deny that Banks had suffered from Rheinfelder's syndrome, though this might well have been the case. As Sir Gordon of course knew, the condition was easily diagnosed by the varying heart beats, but was extremely difficult to detect after death. Certainly the specimens of circulatory tissue showed signs of straining, characteristic of the complaint, to account for the rapid internal bleeding, and it appeared unlikely that any inorganic agent had been responsible for this.

There were, however, certain other features which were puzzling, to say the least. The amines appeared to have become unbalanced, the capillaries were dilated, and there were signs that the vaso-dilator nerves had been dehydrated at the time of death. In a personal footnote the chemist suggested that an unidentified enzyme might have been responsible for these disturbances, and wondered if the deceased could have taken an enormous overdose of some anti-histamine drug. But this was a private opinion and he could not commit himself professionally.

'I should damn well think not.' Sir Gordon spoke aloud to his reflection on the polished desk. Unidentified enzyme indeed! Anti-histamine! Dehydration! Did they consider poor Banks had died of thirst when it was a simple matter of an internal haemorrhage aggravated by the syndrome? He'd told the coroner that, and the centre had certainly taken a long time to send in their report. He had no intention of going back on his opinion now, and Erich Beck could take a running jump at himself. He, Sir Gordon, was the county pathologist, he knew his business, and Banks had suffered from Rheinfelder's syndrome. The fact that Dr Singh with his degree from some tin-pot university in East Pakistan had failed to detect the symptoms was neither here nor there. Sir Gordon picked up the offending document, tore it into four pieces and dropped them into his waste-paper basket. As far as he was concerned the case of George Banks was closed.

* * *

'Not the sort of neighbourhood where one would expect to find a great heiress, Mr Wilde, and I do mean great. The Ecclesiastical Commissioners are shrewd investors and the Railstone trust must be worth a packet by now.' Vincent Buller smiled acquisitively as Marne's Rolls Royce turned into the soul-destroying thoroughfare that was Anderson Road, Fulham. The area was not a slum and not even decayed, but it had remained unaltered. No blocks of flats, towering office buildings or supermarkets had replaced the mean rows of shops and modest Edwardian houses, and the traffic and television aerials were the chief signs that sixty years had passed since Anderson Road came into existence.

'Providing she is the genuine heiress, Mr Buller.' Though John replied to Buller he looked at Marne, feeling quite certain that Marne would have no compunction in producing a false claimant if everything else failed. What a strange man Desmond Marne was, he thought. On the surface, so cynical; probably a multi-millionaire with business interests ranging from heavy engineering to textiles as well as chemicals, but who still referred to himself as a manufacturer of beneficial stinks. As if in answer to John's thoughts, the car drew up at traffic lights alongside a shop front bearing an advertisement for 'Rover's Romp'. Thanks to Marne and his collection of faint odours, undetected by the human, but absorbing to the canine race, the tired pet owner could rest in peace. No longer need he slog up to the park of an evening or be tugged around the streets against his will, because one guinea had turned his suburban garden into a dog's paradise. Six little aerosol sprays provided by Marne Chemicals, eight in the twenty-five shilling pack, squirted at strategic points had solved the exercise problem for good and all. By the garage lay the scent of a fox, beside the rubbish heap an attractive bitch had halted, on the dustbin a Great Dane had lifted its ponderous leg. For hour after happy hour Rover would romp from stench to stench while his owners relaxed and the money poured into the coffers of their benefactor, Lord Marne.

Why should such a cynical, inventive man of business have developed his obsession for the dead poet and painter? Marne had shown John the Railstone self-portrait and the inscribed copy of *Sonnets to Martha* with something akin to awe, and he now sat bolt upright on his seat looking at the drab buildings as if he were on his way to visit an oracle.

'Miss Leame is perfectly genuine, Mr Wilde.' The stub of a hand-rolled cigarette joggled like a growth on Buller's lower lip. 'She'll convince any judge or jury but, with a little publicity from you, I don't believe we'll even have to go to court. You've seen the documents, but you'll be far more impressed when you meet the lady herself.' Buller wore a carnation for the occasion and it contrasted horribly with his crumpled suit and stained collar.

'We've been advertising for Railstone descendants for a long time and there's no harm in telling you that we even considered producing a false claimant to break the trust. The genuine article suddenly turned up quite by chance. I spotted some Georgian silver with the Railstone crest in a Chelsea shop, and the dealer told me he'd bought it from Mrs Atkins, the woman Nancy lives with. I went round to the house merely looking for information and they produced the family tree and the other evidence. But it was Nancy herself who convinced me that I'd hit the jackpot. You'll soon realize she's no impostor, Mr Wilde; you too, Lord Marne. The poor creature is so ill-informed that she hadn't even heard of the trust and didn't know where Caswell Hall was. It took me a good hour to persuade her she was an heiress, and now "power drunk" is the only way to describe her feelings.' The car stopped before a drab terraced house and Buller waited for the chauffeur to open the door.

'Not much of a place, is it? On my first visit I felt rather like Saul looking for asses and stumbling on a kingdom.' He got out, crossed the pavement and adjusted his carnation as he mounted the steps and rang the doorbell.

'Do come in, gentlemen.' A thin, middle-aged woman wearing an apron led them through a narrow hallway and into an overfurnished sitting-room, looking nervously from one face to the other as Buller made the introductions.

'My employer, Lord Marne, Mrs Atkins. Mr John Wilde of the *Daily Globe*, whose articles I'm sure you have read.' Mrs Atkins obviously had read them and there was a copy of the *Globe* on a table to prove it. To an uninformed person the room might have appeared ugly and full of junk. But a collector of Victoriana would have rejoiced at the samplers and the Kate Greenaway prints on the walls, the case of wax fruit on the piano and the life-sized ebony figure of a negress acting as a tray rack.

'Miss Leame is not here, madam?' Marne was perched on the edge of a chaise longue, threadbare and sagging but worth at least a hundred pounds as it stood and perhaps two hundred after it had been re-upholstered. His expression reminded John of a punter with his shirt on an outsider that has not yet arrived in the parade ring.

'Nancy is upstairs, sir. I wanted to have a private word with you, so I told her to go and change her dress when I saw the car draw up.'

'Good, excellent.' Marne was rubbing his hands together. 'Mr Buller has put you in the picture, I understand. Nancy realizes she is going to be a rich woman in the near future?'

'Yes, sir, and that's what I wanted to talk about, because quite frankly it's got me worried.' Mrs Atkins fiddled with a china ornament on the mantelshelf. 'Nancy is a good girl. I was a friend of her mother's and we've shared this house for almost fifteen years now. But excitement isn't good for her. People with dropsy have a lot to put up with and, besides that, Nancy's a bit funny up here.' She tapped her forehead. 'I've never known her so excited as when you left us, Mr Buller.'

'My dear lady, please don't worry about anything.' Buller's voice purred with reassurance. 'We know that Nancy has been a mental patient from time to time and I can promise that the court will be gentle with her. My guess is that we'll win the case without her having to go into the witness box.'

'That's the point, sir, that's the whole point. I'm not worried about her losing the case, but about winning it.' The ornament rattled as Mrs Atkins replaced it on the shelf. 'A quiet life, poor Nancy's had, Mr Buller. Hardly any friends, certainly not a boy friend, kept in the background and only me to take much interest in her. But now, all this has gone to her head. She seems to think that she's a great lady already. Always looked up to me, Nancy did; used to call me Auntie, but now I might be her servant. I don't know where it's going to end and that's a fact.' From the room above boards creaked, there was the sound of a door opening and closing, and heavy feet moving across the landing.

'It can end in nothing but good, Mrs Atkins.' Marne was on his feet, staring towards the doorway and listening to the approaching footsteps. They had left the landing and were coming down the stairs, slow and heavy and without a spring in them, moving carefully from stair to stair, as if their owner's sense of balance was defective and she feared a fall. On and on the steps came, crossing the hall just as slowly and carefully, and then stopped.

'Didn't I tell you that the resemblance was uncanny?' Buller chuckled, but Marne and John hardly heard him. Nancy Leame stood framed in the doorway and her appearance had startled both of them. The photograph had shown the heavy shapeless body, the slack mouth and the red hair and the general air of neurosis, but it had missed a great deal, because heredity had played one of its strangest tricks. Behind the mask of blotchy skin, the coarse features and the troubled eyes, the face of Martin Railstone was looking back at them.

'Lord Marne, Mr Wilde. I had hoped you would have brought a solicitor with you.' She bowed coldly but ignored Marne's outstretched hand. 'There is not much time left for me to claim my inheritance, so let's get on with it.'

Seven

'EVERYTHING all right, Watkins?' Sergeant Major Crawford, late of the Brigade of Guards, now chief 'Prot-Corps' officer at Caswell Hall, was making his evening tour of inspection.

'Quiet as the grave, Sarge.' Crawford's subordinate brought his heels crashing together and gave a mocking salute. He was a student working through the long vac and, though 'Prot-Corps' paid well, he found that time lay very heavy on his hands. 'I only wish something would happen. The Church of England may be as rich as Croesus, but I never knew they threw money away.'

'That's none of your business, Watkins. Just remember that they are paying you and keep your eyes skinned.' Crawford rightly suspected the boy of mickey-taking. 'And watch your lip, my lad. The correct way to address me is Sergeant Major, Mr Crawford, or sir, so don't come the acid.' Crawford moved off, a truncheon jutting from his belt and a large black Labrador named Betty lumbering behind him. They looked a formidable pair, but being a 'Prot-Corps' guard was not a popular occupation and the company had to take what labour it could get. An Arab grenade had scooped out Crawford's right bicep and left him slightly deaf, while Betty, though still strong and active, was getting on in years.

Young Watkins was right, of course, and it did seem a precious waste of money. Just because one lunatic had cut his way into the vault and been killed, there was no need to suppose that another would follow his example, Crawford thought as he turned a corner and saw the lights at the mouth of the valley come into sight. The contractors were working round the clock to beat the weather, and there was a steady hammer of pile-drivers on the slight breeze.

The Bison must be losing his grip. Crawford had served with Norseman and felt warmly towards him as a fellow martinet, but all these precautions appeared pointless. A tumbledown house which was going to be buried under the reservoir whatever happened. The tomb of some crazy nobleman who died a couple of centuries ago. Why pay 'Prot-Corps' almost two hundred quid a week to guard the place? Absurd. Norseman wasn't all that old either; cracking up before his time; premature senility; possibly some mental trouble; poor bleeder; very sad.

'Come on Betty, you idle old bitch. The job's as boring for me as it is for you, so let's get on with it.' He tugged at the lead and the dog whimpered before reluctantly increasing her pace.

'Yes, I know it's a creepy place. But Duty is a stern mistress, as that little pup Watkins remarked yesterday; him thinking I don't know my Shakespeare.' Crawford scowled at the Hall, which looked pleasant enough in daylight but was distinctly sinister in the dusk. By some trick of acoustics, the noise of the pile-drivers seemed to be coming from its walls as though a metallic heart was beating away inside them. He glanced at his watch and made a decision. There was some point in guarding the place during the day when the conducted tours were in progress. Those damn silly newspaper articles had aroused a lot of morbid interest and only yesterday he'd caught a chap who had left his group and was ripping out a piece of carved panelling as a souvenir. But this night duty was just plain nonsense. He'd take a quick look inside and then nip over to the lodge and have a smoke with Syd Smith, the guide.

'Will you keep to heel, Betty?' The dog whimpered again as a deep detonation rumbled up the valley. 'There's nothing to be afraid of; only the workmen blasting away an outcrop of rock.' Crawford unlocked the door and stepped into the house, tugging the Labrador behind him. Her conduct puzzled him slightly because, though she was old and foolish, he hadn't imagined she was a coward.

No, not at all a nice house, he thought. Musty and damp and decayed, of course: that was to be expected. But there was also an atmosphere of sadness and despair which seemed to tell him that even when it was occupied Caswell Hall had been an unpleasant place to live in. Not that he paid any attention to Syd Smith's tales of ghosts and monsters. Crawford's torch flitted along the floors and walls as he moved from room to room and down one dismal corridor to the next. The pile-drivers had fallen silent and his feet rang heavily on the bare boards and flagstones. But as he stepped into what Smith referred to as the ante-chamber, the house trembled with another blast of dynamite.

'Heel, you great useless brute.' The Labrador was straining against the leash and it took all his strength to tug her forward towards the iron cage which guarded the tomb. He shone his torch over the lock and the bars and the stone slab inside, and then turned to go, the dog pulling him now, and her whimpers changing to howls of sheer terror. The rock seam the contractors were blasting must extend right under the foundations, and at the third explosion he distinctly saw one of the bars of the cage quiver. He didn't hear anything to distress him, though. The Labrador's panic-stricken howls were too loud for that, and he let her drag him away, feeling both irritated and worried. He had grown fond of Betty, and if she was becoming gun-shy or subject to fits, she'd have to be destroyed, that was certain.

Once the door was locked behind them however, she quietened down and he put the incident out of his mind. But if Crawford had been alone, if his dog had remained silent, if his hearing had been a little keener, he would have heard the same mocking, threatening laughter which George Banks had experienced.

*   *   *

Everything was going to be all right. Everything he had done was justified. Nothing had been in vain. Lord Marne raised a glass of brandy to the Railstone self-portrait and toasted both his hero and himself, because victory was in sight.

It seemed like yesterday when he had first come across a copy of *The Inner Darkness*, had begun to read, and then read and read and read. Before that moment he had confined his reading of poetry to the major figures and he had felt mild curiosity at first and then growing excitement as the flamboyant, sometimes hysterical, often undisciplined stanzas flowed before his eyes. Martin Railstone had appeared to speak to him personally, giving him more feeling for nature than Wordsworth had done, more concern with sex and death than Yeats, more sadness and longing and hope than he had found in Tennyson. Railstone's verse had awakened Marne like a great crescendo of sound, and after the verse his paintings and his works of scientific scholarship convinced him that the man was one of the greatest geniuses the world had ever produced.

Yes, poet, artist, scholar and scientist. Perhaps a devil, but did that matter when compared to his achievements? The published works had been produced during a tiny period of Railstone's long life. What did that tomb contain and what had he been working on towards the end of his career?

Well, they would know soon enough. Apart from Buller, two independent experts had examined Nancy Leame's credentials and were prepared to swear that they were genuine. Though the Caswell vault story had been driven from the front pages by a sensational murder trial and an air disaster, John Wilde had done a good job, and public interest and pressure was still there. That afternoon in the House of Lords he himself had put a question to the Archbishop of Canterbury and seen him flush and hesitate before giving the evasive answer that 'he would discuss the matter with Dr Norseman and his own legal advisers.' His Grace could discuss it till the cows came home for all the good it would do, because he, Desmond Marne, had got him by the short hairs. However quickly the dam builders worked, however adamant the Dean and Chapter remained, Nancy Leame owned the key to the vaults and she was going to open them.

Marne lit a cigarette and considered the woman's character. Buller had thought her a fool and Mrs Atkins said she was mentally disturbed. They were both right, but Nancy was something else – a visionary like himself, who had accepted her new role with utter conviction. She had never studied the family documents, she had known nothing of the Railstone trust, she had never heard of Caswell Hall, but once Buller had told his story, once she had read John Wilde's articles, her whole personality had altered. Nancy's life had been a dull prison of ill health, loneliness and boredom, and her only friend had been Mrs Atkins. With the material evidence and her uncanny resemblance to Railstone, no judge or jury would reject her claim, and Nancy was already enjoying the inheritance in her mind. The kitchen drudge had been revealed as the lost heiress; the princess had thrown off the goose-girl's rags and claimed her kingdom. Marne personally considered that Mrs Atkins was correct in thinking that Nancy's sudden taste of power and self-importance would eventually lead to her complete insanity, but that didn't worry him in the slightest, because as far as he was concerned she was just a tool.

'Well, did you see them?' He turned as the door opened and Buller came into the room. 'Will we have to go to court, or are they going to be reasonable?'

'They were as reasonable as two such exalted gentlemen can ever be.' Buller's normally cultivated voice was slurred and his feet dragged on the carpet. 'Sir Basil Cloudsley and Mr Norman Spence, legal advisers to the Ecclesiastical Commissioners and the Archbishopric of Canterbury: God rot the bastards. They treated me as if I was a bad smell.' He lurched over to the cocktail cabinet and helped himself to a large cigar and a very, very large whisky.

'But however lordly they may sound, they won't make us go to court, oh dear no. Just think of the publicity the Church would get if it tried to hold a poor sick woman back from her inheritance.' Buller gulped down his whisky and belched loudly as he refilled the glass.

'Cloudsley asked for an interview with Nancy before he makes a final decision. Probably hopes she'll agree to a cash settlement and forget about the house. A fat lot of hope he has there. On the subject of her sainted ancestor, Nancy has become as crazy as you

are.' He lit his cigar and blew a cloud of smoke towards the por-
trait of Railstone.

'Christ, what an ugly little monster the man was. Look at his
grey skin and his swollen limbs and –'

'Shut your mouth.' For a full two years Marne had controlled
his dislike of Buller and now, with victory assured, it came to a
head. He suddenly heard the roar of crowds, and smelled the
sweat and sawdust of the fairground rings where, as a boy, he had
fought with men far heavier and stronger than himself, saving each
purse to buy an education.

'Control yourself, you filthy, slobbering, worthless, drunken
fool, or I'll throw you out of the house myself!'

'Worthless, you say. Fool, you say.' Buller was past caring about
Marne's anger. 'Yes, I'm drunk all right. Why not? Shouldn't the
loyal servant celebrate his master's success? Aren't I the one who
found Nancy and did all the other dirty work for you? Worthless
fool indeed! No, you're the fool, my lord – or perhaps maniac
would be the better word. I'll leave your house all right, but I'll
take my cheque with me. Two thousand was what we agreed on
for the final payment.'

'Two thousand is correct.' Marne fought to push the roar of the
crowd out of his head, and gripped the arms of the chair to control
his hands. 'But we also agreed that payment would not be made
until the tomb had been opened.'

'Oh yes, the tomb. Always the precious tomb of your super-
man, or super-devil.' Buller lurched across to the painting. 'You
once told me that you believed those stories about him might be
true, but you didn't care. Perhaps the Dean and old Bishop Renton
were right all the time. Perhaps there is something hellish in those
vaults. Poor old Renton; such an all-rounder he was in his prime;
so much pleasure he gave me.' Maudlin tears trickled out of
Buller's eyes. 'How could I have done such a thing? How could you
have made me do it, just for that little twisted monster?' He stood
swaying before the picture, took another gulp of whisky and then
threw the glass straight into the painted face of Martin Railstone.

Marne hit him. The bell had rung, the seconds had left the ring
and he was out of his corner with the crowd urging him on. His

right fist crashed against Buller's chin, his left sank into the abdomen and then jabbed up against the heart. He went on hitting him till the man sank back against the wall. The roar of the crowd stopped as if a radio had been switched off, and he drew back shuddering. It was a very long time since Marne had lost control of himself, and this sudden display of convulsive violence horrified him.

'Thank you, my lord. You were quite right to hit me, though you did it for the wrong reason.' Buller half sat, half lay on the floor with the cigar smouldering beside him, and whisky was dripping from the picture frame on to his head.

'Poor, poor old Dud Renton, as they called him. I saw him make a hundred and eighty at Nottingham once and take five wickets for thirty-two runs. What a cricketer Dud was.' The words came in gasps and blood had joined the tears on his face. 'But because I was weak, because the story of Little Boy Blue had driven you insane, you sent me to Dublin to find those two Irishmen to kill him.'

Eight

'MY DEAR William, we have been friends for many years and I do appreciate your feelings.' The Archbishop was old and his voice so faint that Norseman had to hold the telephone hard against his ear to hear him distinctly.

'It has been decided that David Sommerlees will be the next Bishop of Lanchester, but he is lecturing in the States, as you know, and cannot be enthroned till early in November. That means that you must remain in charge of the diocese, and it will be your responsibility to fulfil the Railstone trust and hand over Caswell Hall to Miss Leame.'

'Your Grace, you cannot ask me to do this thing.' Norseman's left hand drummed steadily on his desk and he spoke very slowly and carefully.

'I believe in evil, sir. Not Milton's picturesque Satan, of course, or a stage devil with horns and a cloven hoof and a forked tail. But I am convinced that a force of intentional wickedness exists in the universe, resisting the will of the Creator and keeping this world the hell it partly is. I also believe that this force can become lodged in certain places and people, like dry rot in a building, or a virus in the human body. We all know houses that are bright and sunny, but contain an atmosphere which makes them horrible homes to live in. We also know people who hurt for the pleasure of hurting. No, I have expressed myself badly. Not pleasure, because sadism is at least a positive vice, while their aim is negation. People who, perhaps unconsciously, feel that by causing misery to His creatures, they are slighting God himself. I think C. S. Lewis described their master as "the Bent One".

'Please, please let me finish, Your Grace.' The Archbishop had tried to interrupt and the Dean raised his voice. 'Bishop Renton felt the same as I do, and for the same reason. In his files I came across a manuscript diary written by Railstone himself.'

'It was obviously one of the documents he intended to have buried with him, but was somehow overlooked and given to the bishop for safe keeping.

'Your Grace, that book may have been written by a genius; I am no judge of literature, but I do know that it is the work of an intensely wicked man. His own pen has convinced me that Martin Railstone became possessed by some force of spiritual evil, hostile to both God and mankind, and that it would be a terrible thing to open the vaults and make public his other writings. If you would only read the diary yourself, I am sure you will agree with me.'

'Listen to me.' The old voice might be tired and feeble, but there was a lot of authority in it. 'We are not living in the Dark Ages, and if we have faith there is no need for us to fear the written word, however misguided its author may have been. As Christians we believe that the soul is immortal, but as modern men we know that the body perishes. There is nothing to be frightened of in that tomb, and Caswell Hall must be handed over to its rightful owner in the immediate future. Yes, though I appreciate your views, William, that is my firm wish. Our legal advisers have interviewed Miss Leame and experts have studied the documents. Her claim to the house is perfectly valid and under Railstone's will the diocese was merely appointed as a trustee till a genuine claimant could be found. In law we have not a leg to stand on, and if I followed your suggestion and temporized till the valley was flooded, I would merely bring discredit and shame on our whole institution; discredit which the Church cannot afford.' The Archbishop broke off in a fit of dry wheezy coughing, and when he resumed his voice was barely audible.

'That is why I am asking you to help me. As a friend, will you get in touch with Miss Leame's representatives and arrange a date to hand over the house to her?'

'No, Your Grace, I will not.' Norseman shook his head ponderously and his eyes flicked towards an iron safe in the corner of his study. 'You cannot ask me to do something I believe to be wrong. A friend should not urge me to carry out an act which I consider to go against my Saviour's wishes. However, according to the charter of Lanchester Cathedral, my superior can give me an order. You yourself will have to take the cup from me, Your Grace. Only a direct order will force me to hand over that accursed house.'

'Very well, William. It is an order and you will have it in writing tomorrow. I am sorry that an old friend would not help me of his own free will.' There was another spasm of coughing and a croaked goodbye.

For a long time Norseman sat motionless at his desk, listening to the busy tick of a little French carriage clock on the mantelshelf. Then, as the clock struck ten p.m., he got up, opened the safe and drew out Railstone's diary. He had not looked at it for several days. Not only its revelations, but the very feel and smell of the musty pages sickened him. But he had to know exactly what he was up against before carrying out the Archbishop's orders.

> Caswell Hall. May 10th, 1767. The work on my resting place is finished at last, the Italians have left and the guardians are in position: two to defend the walls and one stationed by the slab. There will be no risk to the woman for whom I am waiting because only male hands would attempt to move that block of basalt.
>
> But it is my body itself that shall be my true guardian, and beside it shall lie a record of all I have done in these

long years, and all I have discovered. Also the orb from which knowledge came; its fellow remains undisturbed in the tomb of Vulfrum.

An orb. The tomb of Vulfrum. Norseman raised his eyebrows. Mary Carlin might be correct in thinking that some medieval relic existed in the vaults. Still, that was unimportant; it was the record that concerned him: evidence to show that Railstone had indeed made a pact with evil.

Tradition suggested that the relics existed and that they had once formed part of a single object. But it was the monastic records of this house, which must also be locked in the vault, that persuaded me to have one of them removed from the cathedral at Lanchester; my piety allowing its fellow to remain there in peace.

For a full year I had no suspicion how great a possession I had obtained; then, one day, I heard mention of the sign-writing of ancient Egypt, and after much patient study the secret was revealed. The gods had sent me the very stuff of life itself if I had the faith and courage to accept it.

The rest of the page was too faded and stained for Norseman to read, and the next entry started in the middle of a sentence.

. . . all because of the gritty wine of creation. My youth was restored, hands guided my brush and my pen, and the voice was always there telling me of the great city that shall rise again if I can but find a person to receive and spread the power which has been lent to me for so short a time. It is clear that the elixir has become part of my body and only one with my malady and colouring, perhaps of my race too, can taste of it and not die. My approaching death persuades me that a woman must be my succes- sor. If only Joan were married or was less puritanical. If only I could find one of the many bastards I have surely fathered.

More indecipherable pages followed, a large section of the book had come loose or been torn out, and the next legible passage was dated a few weeks before Railstone's death.

> The Passion of the Nazarine approaches and soon I must sleep. So evil has my reputation grown that my domestic staff is reduced to three, none of my neighbours will come near me, and travellers between Lanchester and the coast use the longer route rather than pass by this house. But I have no regrets. I experimented upon myself, so why not upon others? Surely the appointed one must come, even if I wait a thousand years, because so many have died in my search for her; Kate and Barbara, General Lockie and the enslaved drabs of the London stews.

The words sloped erratically across the pages and Railstone had clearly been very ill when he wrote them.

> It is the evening of Good Friday. I must wait like a lover pining for his beloved, a servant longing for his mistress, because my own servant is already on his way to the bishop with my testament. His Lordship is an ignorant pedant, but at least an honest man who will guard the trust till she comes to claim it. Till then, all must remain hidden, lest boors and superstitious fools destroy my discoveries out of fear and folly. So patiently I shall wait, and beside me shall lie the sacred thing. Merlin and Arthur and Percival searched for it, Rufus and Stephen held it, but only I, Martin Railstone, a small, sick and ageing man, discovered what it really was.

The writing came to an end and was followed by five words in another and firmer hand. 'God rest his evil soul.'

Merlin and Arthur and Percival. Norseman stood up and paced the floor, deep in thought. A theory had started to creep into his head, but it was so improbable, so unlikely, so full of superstition that his reason revolted against it. He believed in Grace, in the power of the Holy Spirit, but he had always derided the claims of religious relics and felt himself a gullible fool to consider such a notion. And yet . . . yet . . . yet . . .

The little word of doubt clicked in time with the clock, and the Dean shrugged his shoulders and pulled a volume of Creswell's *Folk Lore of the British Islands* from the bookcase. Yes, here was the reference. He laid the book open on the desk and sat down before it.

> The general belief was that, when approached by anyone not of perfect purity, the object would immediately vanish. This is supported by the chivalric version of Gottfried von Strassburg and by several tales in the Welsh *Mabinogion*, which contains one of the most archaic forms of the story.

The Dean gave a snort of self-disgust for his credulity, and then his eyes fell on the next paragraph.

> According to the fourteenth-century monk, Raymond of Ely, however, there is a different result. 'Shoulde any wight who hath donne sinne horrible and be unshriven finde the moste holie thinge, its poures be changed from goode to evile.'

'No, I am a grown man, not a child to be impressed by fairy tales.' Norseman spoke aloud as he closed the book and lit a cigar in the hope that it would help him to concentrate. But it didn't help at all. Merlin and Arthur and Percival. Watching the smoke drift to the ceiling he was reminded of the illustrations of another book he had loved as a boy. The young prince pulling the sword from the stone, Merlin, old and fierce, with a white beard flowing over a druid's cloak, the knight setting out on his quest. After a while he realized that, however unlikely his suspicions might be, he had to discuss them with a second person. He reached for the telephone directory and looked up Mary Carlin's number.

'No, it's not too late, Mr Dean.' Mary glanced at John Wilde stretched out on her sofa. John had returned to Lanchester that evening and called to take her out for a drink. She had persuaded him to eat his way through a four-course menu and the unaccustomed effort had almost knocked him cold. 'What do you want to talk to me about?'

'First I want to apologize, Miss Carlin.' Embarrassment was clear in Norseman's tone. 'I derided your theory about the existence of a relic the other day. If I was rude, I am sorry.

'The fact is that there is a slight possibility that you could be right: there may be a very holy thing indeed walled up inside those vaults. But before I commit myself, I would like you to be more definite. You spoke about the relic in very general terms, but what do you consider the object actually is?'

'Why should I commit myself, Dr Norseman?' Mary was flushed with excitement, but she kept her voice guarded, remembering his scorn and Mrs Wooderson's smiles of patronage. What on earth had caused him to change his earlier opinion she wondered. 'All I know is that tradition, several medieval records and the evidence of the grave-robber suggest that the thing is a small metal container or orb of delicate craftsmanship and extremely heavy for its size. If you are so curious, why not find out for yourself? After all, you are the one person who prevents the vaults being opened.'

'They will soon be opened in spite of anything I can do, Miss Carlin. Please bear with me. I have already apologized for my rudeness.' The Dean was not used to pleading and he sounded as ill at ease as he felt. 'You have obviously done a great deal of research on the subject and you must have a personal theory about the nature of the relic. Do let me hear it.'

'Very well, though you will only laugh at me, Dr Norseman.' Mary had kept her views quiet for so long that she had developed a hard shell of secrecy. 'Get ready for the joke because, in my opinion, the relic taken from Vulfrum's tomb may be a sealed vessel and the most important physical object in Christian tradition.' She raised her voice so that John could hear her as well as Norseman.

'I mean the cup of the Last Supper, the Holy Grail itself.'

Nine

THE Grail, the Sangrail, the Gradalis, the vessel that had been filled with wine and passed from one disciple to another: John tried to remember what he knew of the story.

Following the Last Supper, Joseph of Arimathaea had preserved the bowl and held it beneath the tortured figure on the cross, replacing wine with blood. Then the vessel had been sealed and taken for safety to Britain, the most distant province of the Roman Empire. After that, the object had vanished, now and again appearing in dreams and visions. That was the legend that had sent the knights out on their quest – Galahad and Bors and Percival le Galois; the dream which had inspired the troubadors and set the monkish chroniclers to work. A very beautiful story, John admitted, but only a story. The notion that the chalice had fallen into the hands of Martin Railstone, that Railstone had opened and drunk from it, and that his body had absorbed its powers, transforming them from good to evil, was not only ludicrous, but repugnant.

Why was everybody obsessed by the career of Martin Railstone? Mary lived in a bungalow ten miles to the south of Lanchester, and during each minute of the journey to the Dean's house, John had asked himself that. Until recently he had been tolerantly sceptical about the whole business, but he was changing his opinion. Why should the man's story and his work unbalance the most level-headed mind?

George Banks had not been level-headed, of course. But surely his mental disturbance was not enough to account for his actions? A minor government official who lived quietly in Putney with a widowed sister, drank two half-pints of beer of an evening, never more nor less, and spent his holidays hill-walking in Wales or the Lake District. What pressure had driven such a man to try his hand at grave-robbery?

Erich Beck, eminent scientist, medical historian and suspected war criminal who might have got away with his crimes. John was convinced that Beck had a great deal to hide. Beck obviously believed that there had been some physical cause for Railstone's sudden up-thrust of genius, and the search for that cause had made him as irrational as Banks had been.

Desmond Marne, Marjorie Wooderson and the senior members of the Caswellites, on the surface sane and practical human beings, but fanatics where Railstone was concerned. Why? Was the man's work so very, very brilliant, John wondered. Did the poems and the paintings have some mysterious quality which he himself was unable to appreciate? He had read the *Sonnets to Martha* and visited the Railstone Collection at the National Gallery, and he agreed with the opinions of most critics. Railstone's verse struck him as having force, but little control: rather as if a talented amateur had tried to express deep mystical experience but lacked real ability. 'A poor man's Emily Brontë' was how one eminent don had described him.

There was certainly force in the paintings too. Strange, eerie landscapes with figures that might or might not represent human beings or animals because they were all merged against natural objects. Self-portraits of the artist, each leaving the impression that Railstone was looking towards someone just beyond the edge of the canvas. A lot of imagination had been at work, but Turner would have given the landscapes much more depth and liveliness, and Dali's invention was far more colourful. Still, he was no art or literary critic: perhaps there was some quality he had missed, perhaps Railstone was the God-given genius that his enthusiasts claimed.

Then Mary Carlin, of whom he was becoming very fond. A first-class history graduate who described herself as a feminist, when not actually in bed, and who had once hitch-hiked from Calais to Istanbul on her own. The Grail indeed, the chalice used by Christ Himself and which contained His blood. There was no possible chance that it might be found in the Caswell vaults. Yet not Percival nor Galahad could have looked more eager than did Mary while she pored over the manuscript on the Dean's desk.

Finally, this great 'Bison' of the clerical prairies who had first fought to guard the tomb but now intended to risk his career and possibly his liberty by breaking into it. As John watched Norseman craning over Mary's shoulder he had the uncomfortable feeling that the whole world had gone mad and he was the only sane man left alive.

'We are agreed then. If there is the slightest chance that this holy thing exists, we must take immediate action.' The Dean swung round to John.

'Oh, I know what you're thinking, young man. You wonder what is the urgency? The Archbishop has ordered me to make over the house to Miss Leame, so why not wait for her to open the vaults?

'I will tell you, Mr Wilde.' Though John had not opened his mouth a great, gnarled hand was raised to silence him.

'I am still not entirely convinced that Miss Carlin's theory is true, but if she is right, if the chalice exists, if it has been opened, enormous forces of evil may be contained in that tomb. Nor could I risk the vessel falling into the hands of Marne and the rest of them. While there is breath in my body I shall prevent that.' He expanded his chest to prove the point.

'You are serious about this, sir?' John glanced at Mary for support, but she was watching Norseman with the expression of a dog whose owner has just said 'walk'. 'You intend to enter the tomb and look for the relic? Surely you are running a grave legal risk.'

'Possibly, though until I receive written orders from the Archbishop and signed certain documents I am still in charge of the trust.' Norseman marched over to a sideboard laden with a fine assortment of bottles.

'If there is the very slightest chance that our theory is correct, do you imagine any material considerations would deter me, Mr Wilde? The Sangrail, the very chalice that was used by my Master – do you believe that the law could keep me away from it?' He poured out three generous measures of brandy, handed them their glasses and raised his to Mary.

'To the success of our mission, my dear. I am glad to have you as an ally, even though Mr Wilde continues to wave a white flag and show himself a Doubting Thomas.'

'Extremely doubting, but you can forget the white flag, Dr Norseman. I'm coming with you and just try to stop me.' John sipped at the brandy, already working out his treatment of the story. He should get at least three columns and have a large picture of Norseman scowling out on the front page, frustrated but unrepentant. That would make amusing reading – but how very much better it could be! In spite of himself, John was already starting to share his companions' eagerness. If they were not frustrated, if the incredible happened and the photograph showed Norseman holding a little metal cup . . . No, he forced the very thought of that out of his mind, though excitement remained. 'When will this raid take place?'

'Now, at this very moment, so let's get ourselves prepared.' The Dean finished his drink and crossed to the door of an adjoining room, motioning them to follow him.

'This is my private den. Still a bit of a muddle, because I haven't been in residence very long, but we should find all we need. He had obviously been a keen mountaineer and a collector of battlefield souvenirs, and nodded proudly at the assortment of military and sporting equipment spread out before them. An ice axe lay beside a sub-machine gun, a rope was festooned around a shell case, a scarlet anorak hung from a tripod of rifles with a German helmet perched above it. Beneath a framed photograph of Norseman clinging to a vertical cliff face lay a sinister-looking contraption of cylinders and plastic tubes.

'We'll need this to free the slab, and you'll find a couple of torches in that cupboard over there.' He handed John the ice axe. 'And you take that rope, Mary. If the stairs into the vault are wood, they're bound to have rotted by now. The blighter spoke of guardians, didn't he?' He glanced longingly at the submachine gun and shook his head.

'No, I don't think that would provide any protection, but we'll certainly take you along, my sweet.' He lifted the contraption from beneath his picture and held it out for their inspection. 'Nice, isn't it? A Japanese copy of a German model which I picked up in Burma. Clever little people, the Japs; you can see that it was designed for jungle fighting – it's very light and compact. Not much range or staying power, of course, but it will serve our purpose. Now, all I need is the key to that cage over the slab and we're ready.'

'But I don't understand.' Norseman was swinging the apparatus carelessly in one hand and Mary drew back before the wicked-looking nozzle. 'Isn't that a flame-thrower?'

'Perfectly correct, my dear, and there's no need to be alarmed. The cylinders are empty at the moment, but there's petrol in my garage to remedy that.' He grinned at the astonishment on their faces.

'Oh, I'm not afraid of Railstone's guardians. This is not a weapon to defend us, but a simple sterilizing device; a broom to sweep clean an extremely dirty place. Thanks, Wilde.' He took a torch from John and thrust it into his pocket.

'We are going to Caswell Hall in the hope of finding a very holy thing. We may be frustrated, but I can assure you on one point: when Marne and his jackals finally enter that tomb, do you know what they'll find?

'Ash, Mary; burned refuse, Wilde.' He laughed as he hoisted the flame-thrower on to his shoulders. 'With this little beauty I intend to blast Martin Railstone's legacy from the face of the earth.'

Ten

THERE is nothing to fear in this house. The relic may exist, we may find proof of Railstone's genius, there will certainly be a dead body in the tomb. But nothing can harm us because the dead do not return to life and Martin Railstone died two hundred years ago. Mary attempted to reassure herself as, with her hand in John's, she followed the Dean down the musty corridors of Caswell Hall, but with each step she became more and more frightened.

One summer, when she was very young, Mary's parents had gone abroad and she had stayed with two maiden aunts in the country. She was fond of her aunts, they had a pony for her to ride, a dog to play with and a parrot which actually did talk, and she should have enjoyed her stay with them. But she didn't. She hated every minute of it, because there were rats in the house.

Not that she ever saw a rat or the sign of their presence. But each night when she lay in bed, listening to the London train pull out and longing to be on it, the noises would start. Little rumblings beneath the floor at first, scufflings and screams behind the skirtings, then the sound of teeth steadily gnawing their way through a board towards her. Her aunts told her she was a silly girl when she cried out for them. They said that the animals would never come into the room because they were much more frightened of her than she was of them and, in any case, a man would be coming to get rid of them very soon. Mary didn't believe a word of it. Even after the rat-catcher had been and gone, she was sure that the menace remained and was merely keeping quiet and waiting to strike. The nights were the worst, but in daytime too the house was a place of terror, and wherever she was, whatever she was doing, playing or eating or reading, she knew that a cunning and hostile intelligence was watching her.

She had a similar sensation now with Norseman's feet pounding on in front of her, John's hand warm and comforting and Crawford, the 'Prot-Corps' guard, bringing up the rear with an electric lantern. There could be no rats in the shell of Caswell Hall – there was nothing for rats to feed on; but from behind every wall and doorway and pillar she felt that eyes were staring at them.

John had no such sensations. He was eager to know what the vaults really did contain and excited at the possibility of a worldwide scoop. But the flame-thrower swinging on the Dean's shoulders made him feel rather guilty at being a party to the expedition. He had not been greatly impressed by Railstone's creations, but if the man really had been the genius his adherents claimed, surely they should be preserved for posterity? When the time came he would have to dissuade Norseman from his witch-burning.

'Here we are, ready to start the good work.' Norseman marched into the ante-chamber and lowered the *Flammenwerfer*, already imagining a great blast of orange and scarlet flame belching from it. The moon was shining directly through one of the stained-glass windows and the multi-coloured beams seemed to be giving a blessing to his enterprise. He was quite without anxiety, because he knew that God Himself was on his side and he had not the slightest sense of guilt. He felt like a crusader about to rescue a holy thing and wipe out evil. If Railstone had indeed opened that cup and drunk from it, the blasphemy was unspeakable and complete goodness might have been turned into a force of destruction. If the man had been a genius, so had Hitler. If his written works showed brilliance, so did de Sade's. Art and science and literature were unimportant compared with spiritual corruption, and the Dean's profession was the cure and salvation of souls.

'Let's have some light on the subject, Sergeant Major.' He motioned Crawford forward and the bars of the cage showed black and massive in the light of the lantern. The blasting operations had stopped, but pile-drivers were still hammering away in the distance.

'The fellow employed good honest workmen, whatever his faults.' The Dean studied the ironwork, then took a key from his pocket and fitted it into the lock.

'Rusted solid, as was to be expected, but let's see what a bit of elbow grease will do.' He flexed his muscles, but the lock remained adamant.

'No, I don't think you'd better try levering it with the axe, Wilde. This is the only key in existence, to the best of my knowledge, and you might break the shank. Give it a good dollop of oil, Sergeant Major.' He shone his torch into the cage while he waited for the oil to penetrate, and they all stood looking down at the carved slab, with their different thoughts.

Don't be a fool. There is nothing to be frightened of. Once again Mary tried to reassure herself. Behind that stone may lie the most important religious relic in the world and you will have helped to reclaim it. Martin Railstone can't hurt anyone. He died centuries ago and his body will be dust and dry bone. George Banks was delirious when he talked about the laughter, so pull yourself together.

If the chalice is there, I'll have made one of the biggest scoops in history and I'm going to ask Mary to marry me. I think I love her: I know I like her far more than any woman I've ever met. John pulled out his flashbulb camera and took a shot of her and Norseman.

But can the relic exist? Even if there is a chalice in the vaults, could it possibly be the Grail? Surely metal drinking vessels were very expensive at the time and only earthenware crockery would have been used at the inn in Jerusalem?

Why should the dog have behaved like that? Crawford was wondering. Couldn't have been the blasting because that went on after we left the house and she was perfectly quiet then. Everybody seems to have gone barmy tonight. What does the Bison think he's going to do with that ruddy flame-thrower? Must be completely round the bend. I know he's the one who's paying the company, but I hope I've done the right thing in letting him in.

How strong was eighteenth-century cement? Norseman considered the technical problems. In the centre of the slab, the phallic boss pointed proudly towards the ceiling at a seventy-degree angle: a symbol of Railstone's legendary virility, challenging him to work facing it. While the slab itself was solid basalt a good nine inches thick which would take an expert quarryman to split, the mortar around the edge looked thin and crumbling.

'That oil should have penetrated by now.' He grasped the key again and this time it turned easily, the heavy tongue drew back and he pulled the door open, its hinges creaking with the rust of the years.

'So far so good: the first barrier is down.' Norseman slipped off his jacket and rolled up his shirtsleeves, showing huge forearms covered with thick blond hair. As he took the axe from John and stepped inside the cage he looked very much like one of his Viking ancestors preparing to split a skull.

'Now, for your second line of defence, Sir Martin. Yes, by all means take my picture, Wilde.' He glowered towards the camera for a moment, then raised the axe above his shoulders and brought it hurtling down with all his strength behind it. The blade met the gap between the slab and the paving stones with a soft, dull thud, and it was clear that the mortar would give him little trouble.

'Soft as putty, but I wonder what's behind it.' The Dean laughed triumphantly and John saw that he enjoyed breaking things. A Norse berserker might have given just such a laugh as he hewed his way into a Saxon keep.

'Ah, I was afraid of that. There is a harder layer.' His second blow had dislodged a large chunk of cement but the axe blade had rung metallically. He crouched down and started to chip away at the gap he had made. 'If I can just extend this enough to get a purchase I might be able to lever the whole slab away bodily.'

'Dr Norseman, stop it. Please come away from the slab.' The feeling of impending danger had become intolerable and Mary couldn't control herself. 'There is something behind that stone. I can sense it: something horrible!'

'Naturally there is. That is one of the reasons why we are here. But there's no need to be neurotic. Just take the torch and hold it steady, there's a good girl.'

'Yes, excellent.' He inserted the flat end of the blade into the gap and bore down on the handle. The metal creaked against the flagstones, gained a fulcrum, and the slab started to move. The first guardian struck.

John was adjusting his camera at the time and he never saw how it happened, though the crash of metal, Mary's screams and the Dean's sudden bellow of agony brought his face up with a jerk. What he saw then would remain with him for the rest of his life, and later made him remember that an earlier, pre-Christian version of the Grail story described it, not as a cup, but as a spear which dripped with blood. A long bronze shaft held Norseman suspended against the bars of the cage, and the tip of the proud, rampant phallus protruded from between his shoulder blades.

Eleven

BY a miracle Norseman did not die. There had been some enormous engine behind the booby trap and for a full hour his body was held moaning against the cage till hacksaws cut through the bronze shaft and released him. He was unconscious when they finally carried him out to the ambulance and for weeks he remained unconscious while surgeons patched his lung and probed for fragments of bone, and tubes fed nourishment into his veins. The doctors thought he would die, every law of nature stated that he must die, but he proved them wrong. Perhaps it was a subconscious will to live, perhaps a defiance of fate, perhaps an act of God, as he himself considered to be the case when he recovered. Whatever the reasons, the undamaged lung continued to rise and fall, the great, strong heart beat faintly on, and day by day the pale features on the pillow took on a little more colour. Then, in the small hours of one morning, a night nurse saw his eyes open and his lips curve into a smile: William Norseman was out of danger, and Railstone's first guardian had failed. The catch which released that phallic spear had also been a lock and the slab had moved, revealing a three-inch gap with a glimpse of stone stairs behind it.

Nobody went down those stairs, though. Nobody entered the Hall now, though morbid sightseers viewed it from the safety of the road or through the locked gates. Fear of the law and the supernatural had held the vaults in isolation, and now mechanical threats had been added. What other death traps might await interlopers? How many more guardians might Martin Railstone's inventive mind have created to protect his secrets? John's photograph of the Dean transfixed against the cage had been too gruesome for publication, but his eye-witness account had given many of its readers a bad nightmare. For the time being Caswell Hall was shunned like the plague.

Erich Beck did not remain idle, however. Refusing to accept Sir Gordon Lampton's bland denial that the analyst's report on the organs taken from Banks's body contained anything of interest, he called at the research centre and managed to obtain a copy of the findings. When he had studied it, he telephoned John.

'Mr Wilde, you and Miss Carlin have told me that you cannot divulge anything you read in the diary till you have permission from the Dean to do so. I appreciate your loyalty to Dr Norseman, of course, but there is something I must know at once and I am sure Norseman would wish you to tell me if he were not . . . indisposed.' Beck hesitated slightly over the word.

'Was there any suggestion that Railstone might not have been insane when he made the will, but that it was deliberately thought out? For instance, did he give an exact physical description of his heiress?'

'Railstone described her, Professor, but he was clearly insane in my view.' The German had sounded very persuasive and John told him of the passage reading 'the elixir has become a part of my body and only one with my malady and my colouring, perhaps of my race too, can taste of it and not die.'

'Thank you, Mr Wilde. Thank you very much indeed.' John could hear the excitement in Beck's voice. 'I am sure now that Banks died, not merely because of his injuries, nor because he suffered from Rheinfelder's syndrome, as Sir Gordon still imagines. Some unidentified substance disturbed the amines in his bloodstream and that was what killed him. Perhaps he might not have died if he had been a descendant of Martin Railstone.'

'There is nothing supernatural about it, my friend.' Beck gave a slight hiss of impatience at John's question. 'Railstone knew what he was doing when he made that will and it is good practical medicine. Remember that certain illnesses may stimulate both mind and body of the sufferer and that the spores of many bacteria may lie dormant but alive for very long periods of time. Also remember that the blood of one group cannot merge with that of another, and that cell grafting is only completely safe in the case of identical twins.'

'You mean that some form of bacteria was responsible for Railstone's mental activity? That its spores remained dormant in the tomb and Banks became infected by them?'

'Not think. I wonder, Mr Wilde. But I am beginning to believe that the Caswell vaults contain a great danger which might be turned into an even greater benefit to mankind. I am also sure that Miss Leame is the one person who can prove or discredit my theory. As I said, it is just a theory, and I would prefer not to discuss it further. We will just have to wait for Miss Leame to claim her inheritance. Thank you for your information, and I would advise you to put all supernatural notions right out of your mind. Railstone may have possessed the touch of death, but there was a purely physical reason for it. Goodbye, Mr Wilde.'

He rang off, leaving John both frustrated and perplexed, and a further conversation with the lordly Dr Franklin made him no wiser.

The weeks passed and the lawyers grew fat. Marne's representatives claimed that the Archbishop could personally hand over
the estate to Nancy Leame, but legal opinions were divided. The
trust clearly stated that only a Bishop of Lanchester or his Dean
and Chapter could make the transfer, and Norseman was too ill to
be worried; his doctors were adamant on that score. The bishop
designate, David Sommerlees, was enjoying his lecture tour of
the United States and refused to return for enthronement till late
autumn. Marne stormed from solicitor to barrister, and Nancy
Leame, no longer elated with sudden power and self-importance
but sullen and despondent, fretted like some nature goddess whose
worshippers have deserted her for another creed.

It was Buller, repentant and sobered by Marne's fists, who came
up with a solution. The Archbishop wanted nothing better than to
wash his hands of the whole business and Sommerlees was solely
concerned with his lectures, which were bringing him much appro-
bation and applause. Why could not Sommerlees be enthroned in
his absence by a proxy? After a week's costly deliberations Messrs
Cloudsley and Spence discovered that there had been precedents
for this in canon law and gave their agreement. The enthronement
ceremony was rushed through with a nervous minor canon taking
his lordship's role, and the necessary documents were prepared.
Before the end of the month, David Sommerlees sat down in the
ranch house of a Texan oil tycoon and signed 'David Lanchester'
with a flourish.

When he heard the news that the final legal obstacle had been
removed, Marne felt strangely unelated. He handed Buller his
cheque and he toasted Nancy in champagne, but somehow the
battle had gone on for so long that doubts were creeping into his
mind. As he raised the glass towards Nancy, he was again struck
by her uncanny physical resemblance to her ancestor; the red
hair, the dropsy and the clear hint of Railstone's face behind the
slack mouth and the heavy features. But his feelings were quite
different from those he had when he first saw her. He had always
considered Railstone was insane at the end and that megalomania
had prompted him to name an heiress akin to himself in every
way. Could he have been insane for years before he died, perhaps?

Marne was a completely ruthless man. He had arranged Renton's murder and he felt no pity for the Dean, whom he regarded as a personal enemy. But that booby trap which had transfixed Norseman hinted at madness. Perhaps all Railstone's best work had been done during that single short period, and the chest would contain nothing but senile ramblings and the daubs of an artist whose talents had deserted him.

Practical problems remained, however, and they gave Marne little time for his anxieties, because the vaults had still to be opened. Nancy claimed the right to be the first person to enter them, and he experienced the bitter, unbalanced tantrums Mrs Atkins had mentioned when he told her that that was impossible. One booby trap had almost killed a man and there would probably be others. Only a specialist could be asked to undertake the job, and such specialists were difficult to find.

The army was Marne's first hope, but it proved a very weak reed. 'Send one of our chaps down there?' A colonel at the Ministry of Defence had frowned and raised his eyebrows. 'My dear sir, this department is concerned with bomb disposal; modern high explosives, not contraptions of two centuries ago. Besides, there's no danger to life or property that I can see, so it's nothing to do with us.

'Oh by all means, visit the Cherfield depot and ask for volunteers. I'll not only give you a chit to the commanding officer, I promise to eat my hat if you find one.'

The underworld was also approached and displayed far more courage. Two old lags who gloried in the titles of Billy the Tunneller and Slippery Sam Watson were discovered by Buller, and offered their services for a decent fee. Marne was hopeful at first, but then learned that the Tunneller had been caught red-handed in six out of his nine jobs, and that Sam might once have been slippery but now suffered from chronic rheumatism.

The stage finally provided the specialist. Charlie Smith, known to his public as Blondin, the Human Eel, looked and moved like a battered rubber ball as he proudly displayed the marks of his calling. He had a broken nose, received after being dropped from the Forth Bridge in a beer barrel. The scars on his forearm were acquired while crawling through a drainpipe lined with needle-sharp spikes. The slight limp had been produced by a charging buffalo when he was working as a stunt man in California. The loss of his little finger had been very unpleasant and also galling, because a namesake was responsible: a conger eel had bitten it off while he was escaping from a weighted sack at the bottom of Folkestone harbour.

Booby traps were no problem to Blondin, because he had a sixth sense to smell them out. For a hundred pounds down and a further two on completion of the contract, he would be only too delighted to lead the way to the tomb. Marne had written a cheque then and there and Blondin had hurried off to make his arrangements.

But time was running out: the Cass River dam was ready. Muscle, machinery and bonus rates of pay had all played their part, and the concrete sections stretched across the valley, buttressed and braced and grouted to contain the water when the weather broke. That would not be long.

The storms that had swept the American coastline for some weeks were moving east and the air liner which had carried the legal documents to Sommerlees had been over two hours late because of head winds. The long hot summer was almost done and the clouds hurried across the Atlantic, gathering more moisture as they came. They met the hills of Ireland and Wales, creating havoc to crops and buildings, and swept on with undiminished power. On the day after Marne had spoken to Blondin, they reached the Lanchester area: the wind dropped and the rain came down. It fell in sheets, soaking into the hard, dry earth, filling the streams and the springs and swelling the river which met the concrete wall of the dam and was forced back towards the hollow that contained the Hall. The rain rattled on the roof of the old house and drummed on the lake, which soon started to overflow its banks.

But Sir Martin Railstone gave no sign that he had heard it. He just lay on his stone bed and grinned.

Twelve

ON the day that Norseman resealed the breach George Banks had made, there had been an almost holiday atmosphere surrounding Caswell Hall. Little white clouds had drifted across the blue sky like vapour trails, the sun had lit up the gay robes of the clergy and the bright yellow paint of the concrete tanker and, with the exception of a few fanatics, the crowd had been 'out for a bit of a lark' and generally friendly.

But there was no holiday atmosphere now. Though it was only four in the afternoon, a dark sky hung over the valley and the rain fell straight down through the windless air, swelling the river and rebounding from the surface of the lake like a forest of steel spikes standing upright. It hammered on the television cameras stationed in the car park, on the raincoats and umbrellas of the reporters and the public and the black capes of the police, and it streamed over Marne's shooting brake that stood like a waiting hearse before the doorway.

'Yes, chaps, it is unfair and I am privileged.' John grinned at a group of his colleagues who were clamouring around him and Mary as a police sergeant examined the pass Marne had given them. 'It's been my story from the word go, remember. Come on, Mary. We're late already.'

The policeman stood back to allow them to pass, and for the last time they hurried down the long corridors leading towards the ante-chamber of the tomb. 'And don't worry. Nothing will go wrong today. Trust Marne to find an expert: this chap Smith is supposed to be about the best in the business. Just keep praying that your relic really does exist. If it does I'll have the biggest scoop since printing was invented and you'll be in the history books whether you like it or not.'

But though John smiled, he didn't really expect that the relic would be found, and the atmosphere before the passage leading to the ante-chamber confirmed his doubts. Very few people had

been allowed in the house and except for Blondin and his assistants
– a gangling youth and a stout blonde, both dressed in red plastic
overalls – who obviously intended to treat the business as a theatrical performance, there was an air of drab anti-climax hanging over
the gathering. Mrs Wooderson stood chatting to a solicitor and a
tall clergyman who represented the diocese, and Marne and half a
dozen of the more prominent Caswellites were stationed around
Nancy Leame and Mrs Atkins as if protecting their patroness.
Erich Beck, looking pale and anxious, had somehow persuaded Sir
Gordon Lampton to be present, and Sir Gordon stood beside him
surveying the scene with lordly contempt.

'I'd get started, if I were you, Smith.' The reservoir contractors
had also sent a representative, a dour Scotsman who spoke with
a pipe stuck in the corner of his mouth. 'The rainfall has been
heavier than anything I've ever experienced in southern England
and the hollow is filling up fast. In my estimation it will be unwise
for you to remain in the house after seven o'clock, and highly dangerous after eight.' He produced a large turnip watch and nodded
coldly. 'That gives you just under three hours.'

'Which we won't need, Mr . . . whatever your name is, and I
prefer to be addressed by my professional title when I'm working.
We 'ave everything ready, studied the layout of the building and
it'll be an hour's work at the outside.' Blondin had been adjusting
a light portable winch and he now tied a grappling hook to the end
of its line.

'Your attention please, ladies and gentlemen.' He gave a theatrical bow, as though imagining he were on a stage. 'I am now
about to remove the first obstacle and I will ask you to wait here
for a very short period of time because it won't take a jiff. And you
watch yourself, Sir Martin Railstone. The Human Eel is about to
wriggle into your private parts. Oh, sorry, mum, I meant private
vaults, of course.' Blondin was used to pretty low audiences and he
rolled his eyes at Mrs Wooderson's frown of disgust before hurrying off with the grapple in his hand.

'It's all right, dear. Don't get excited.' Mrs Atkins was patting
Nancy's arm and soothing her as though she were a frightened
child. 'There's nothing to be frightened of.'

'Of course there's nothing to be frightened of, Ethel. This house is mine, all mine, every brick and stone of it.' Her eyes darted round the ramshackle room with great pride of possession. 'My ancestor left it to me. He knew that one day I would come to claim it, so why should I be frightened of him when he's waiting for me?' Nancy pulled away from her friend and walked across to Mary. 'You understand that, don't you, Miss Carlin? Sir Martin promised that he wouldn't die till I came. That's the truth, isn't it? He wrote it in one of his poems.'

'That is what he implied, Miss Leame.' Mary felt slightly saddened by the complete conviction in the woman's voice, and she wondered how much of it came from her own imagination and how much Marne and the others had influenced her. If the tomb contained nothing of any importance, Nancy Leame would be a very distressed woman indeed.

'Here goes, Linda.' The line had been given a sharp tug and Blondin's assistants bent over the handles of the winch. The ratchet clanked steadily as the line was drawn in and, from the distance, there came a heavy scraping sound. A moment later Blondin reappeared, bowing again and showing a lot of gold in his smile.

'Easy as falling off a log so far, ladies and gents, though who knows what further surprises the old gentleman has prepared for your entertainment? Follow me and we'll find out.' With another bow and another flash of gold bridging he led them forward towards the ante-chamber.

His assistants had removed most of the cage earlier in the day, but the upper sections of the bars still protruded from the ceiling, their ends rounded like fangs by the acetylene cutter. The winch had dragged the slab aside to reveal a flight of stone steps leading down into the darkness and a series of bronze levers balanced on pivots: the engine which had driven the phallic spear through Norseman's body.

'Narsty that, ladies and gents. Obviously activated by lead weights and, as the mechanism's bronze, rust wouldn't affect it. Release a catch by movin' the slab, down go the weights and up the bleeder comes.' Blondin's voice had become more cockney as he stared through the opening.

'What's that, miss?' He held out an arm as Nancy Leame pushed forward. 'No, ducks, sorry to block a lady's passage, but I don't care if the house is your property. No one's goin' down that 'ole till I've made sure it's all safe and sound.

''Urry up now. You know I don't like 'anging abaht.' He waited impatiently for his assistants, who were attaching two long flexible shafts to a metal roller.

'Right. Stand well back all of you, now. This is where we could 'ave a spot o' bother.' Blondin still smiled automatically, but his face was tense as he wheeled the roller to the edge of the first step and very gently lowered it. He might use blue comedy in his act, but he obviously had a healthy respect for the possibilities of death and mutilation.

'Miss Carlin, Mr Wilde.' Beck had crossed over to them and was holding out two plastic packages. 'Before you arrived I spoke to the others and not one of them would listen to me. They are all thinking about booby traps and mechanical devices; even about some supernatural force. They won't even try to realize what the real danger could be.'

'You mean the bacteriological menace you hinted at on the tele-phone? I understand there is little foundation for that, Professor.' John tried not to appear rude, but Franklin had derided any such possibility and Beck's persistence irritated him.

'Possibly, possibly, my friend, but take these just in case.' The German pushed the packages into their hands, as Blondin's roller clanked against another step. 'I am probably just an old fool obsessed by something that happened long ago, but why take chances? These contain muslin masks saturated with disinfectant and they might save your lives. Please put them on if we go down there. Promise me you will do that, Miss Carlin.'

'I promise, Professor.' Though Mary nodded, her thoughts were concentrated on the sound of the roller moving down into the vaults. Would the next step set off a death trap and the metallic clank be drowned by the roar of explosives?

'Thank you, my dear.' Beck turned and walked back to Sir Gordon, who was still regarding the proceedings with a cynical sneer and must have come along merely out of idle curiosity.

'That's that, then. Rock bottom and all's well.' Blondin lowered the shafts. He had clearly regarded the steps as the main danger point and the air of tenseness had left him. 'I must say the old party 'as disappointed me. How long did you say 'e'd been down there, Lord Marne? Two 'undred years, wasn't it? Give us the torch, Linda love, and I'll go and wake the bleeder up.' He took it from her and walked confidently down the staircase.

Nobody spoke, though Marne gave a little grunt of impatience, Marjorie Wooderson coughed and the Scots engineer relit his pipe, the scrape of the match loud against the drumming of rain on the roof. From time to time they could hear Blondin humming as he moved about the room beneath them and now and again the beam of his torch could be seen at the opening. Then the humming stopped, the feet halted, there was a scream, and up from the vaults came the sound that had frightened Banks into panic and maddened the dog.

The laughter was light and soft at first, but it rose to a chuckle, then a cackle, and finally to a great bellow of mirth full of threat and menace. They all drew back before the sound, and to each of them it meant something different. To Mary it was a crone revelling at a crucifixion; to John, a concentration-camp guard mocking his victims; to Erich Beck, a medieval devil enjoying the torments of the damned; to Nancy Leame, schoolchildren jeering at a slow-witted dunce. For perhaps two minutes – but they seemed much, much longer – the laughter rolled up the staircase, then suddenly stopped, as if the creature who made it had been gagged. Another minute passed and Blondin reappeared at the opening. His face was sweating to show that he had had a bad shock, but it was also bright with triumph.

'Cor, if that put the wind up you, just imagine what it done to me.' He pulled out a handkerchief and wiped his forehead. 'A right bastard, the old bleeder must 'ave bin, but there's nothing to 'arm anyone. No ghosts, ladies and gentlemen; no Glamis 'orror, like you wrote about, Mr Wilde; Sir Martin ain't risen from the dead, me lord.

'Take the lantern down, Len, and we'll show them what 'e was up to.' He waved his assistants forward and motioned the rest to follow them. Marne was obviously tense with excitement, Sir Gordon still looked slightly shaken and was without his usual sneer, and Nancy Leame's mouth was wide open and her eyes over-bright, as if she were in a trance. But the majority had smiles of relief from the assurance that the hideous sound must have a natural source. Only Beck appeared really distressed: he had fitted a muslin mask over his face.

''Ere's the laughin' cavalier.' Like the good showman he was, Blondin did not speak till all his audience were assembled. The vault was long and low with a stone floor and ceiling, and appeared strangely free of dust and cobwebs. Beside a door in the opposite wall stood a wooden box about the size and shape of a coffin.

'There you are, that's all there is to it: a mechanical device designed to put the fear of hell into you.' The front of the box was open and the beam of his torch lit up a pendulum, two lead weights and a clockwork motor.

'Very simple and very nasty.' He touched a brass wire threaded through hooks set along the walls and immediately the pendulum started to swing, the clockwork revolved and the obscene chuckles recommenced. Blondin hurriedly stopped the mechanism before it could build up to full power.

'There's another one in the corner over there and obviously a third in the next room; most likely it'll 'ave run down after frightening that pore bloke Banks out of his wits. Metal bellows make the actual noise and the slightest vibrations sets 'em off.'

'Stop talking, man, and look at the water.' Marne was staring at the stream of liquid trickling out from under the door. 'The inner chamber is flooding already, so start breaking the lock. If the material in that chest is damaged, I'll never forgive myself.'

'No need for that, sir. I tried the door myself and it ain't locked. Banks went inside that room, so I shouldn't think there's any danger, but you'd better all stand back by the stairs while I take a dekko.'

'I will not stand back any longer.' Nancy faced him like a rock. 'This is my house, my property and you are only here because I gave you permission. Don't you understand that I have to go into the room on my own, though Lord Marne and Miss Carlin can come behind me? Give me the torch and get out of my way.' He made no move to obey her and she stamped her foot petulantly. 'You are just a paid servant, so do as you are told.'

'Okay, ducks, you're the boss all right, but don't say that I didn't warn you.' Blondin handed her the torch with an arch shrug of the shoulders. 'We must always try to please the ladies, mustn't we?'

'Mary, you are not going with them! And put on the mask, just in case.' John gripped her arm as Nancy Leame started to pull back the door. The hinges were of gunmetal or some other rust-proof alloy, and it opened silently. With Marne at her heels and half a dozen torches lighting their way, Nancy stepped into the last resting place of Martin Railstone.

In several stanzas of *The Inner Darkness* Sir Martin had suggested that he would not die, but he looked dead enough. His body was shrouded, with face and hands exposed, and his arms and legs crossed in the posture of a crusader, while at the foot of the slab which supported him lay a big brass-bound chest. The visible flesh was mummified and curiously perforated, as if woodworm had bored into it, and decayed teeth grinned horribly towards the torches.

'Don't touch him. Don't go near the body if you value your health . . . your lives even!' Beck screamed out the warning, but neither Marne nor Nancy heard him. Marne's hand already lay on one of the mummified claws, and Nancy was bending down towards the grinning death's head as if greeting a lover. As she reached it, her jacket brushed against something on the slab; there was a sharp, metallic click, and Mary's fears left her as her eyes grew wide with awe and wonder.

Lying on the floor – which was already an inch deep in water – was a little, oval, silver-coloured object that gleamed in the torchlight as if the metal that formed it had recently been polished.

Thirteen

For most of her life Nancy Leame had been a crushed nonentity, but she looked like a queen or a priestess when she finally straightened from the corpse.

'You may take the chest and its contents as I promised, Lord Marne, but the body must remain here. No, leave him, I say.' Erich Beck had walked forward and the shroud crumbled in Nancy's hands as she tried to cover the ravaged face.

'My ancestor must have been ill or insane when he dreamed about immortality, so let him rest in peace.' She stooped and lifted the metal object, holding it like the symbol of some religious office for a moment and then slipped it into her handbag and stood silently while Blondin and his assistants prepared for the departure.

The chest was very heavy: the winch was used to drag it up the stairs, and four men carried it coffinwise through the gloomy passages to the front door and the waiting crowd. If anything the rain had increased in volume and the bearers were up to their ankles in water as they hoisted their burden into the back of the shooting brake. Already the moat was filling up, the river and the lake had swollen far beyond their known limits and soon the old house would be under water.

'Did you find anything, Miss Carlin?' 'Give us a chance, dear.' 'Your pal Wilde's had it all to himself so far.' Mary and Nancy had brought up the rear of the party and they were immediately surrounded by reporters as the police cordon closed in to protect the brake. 'Were there any more booby traps down there? Any of these monsters we've been hearing so much about? Come on, Miss Leame, let's hear about it.' Flash bulbs exploded, and the surging crowd of journalists had forced them away from their companions.

'*Daily Star* here, girls, so let's have your story . . .' 'Did you see the body, Nancy . . . ?' 'Was he barmy when he said he'd come to life? . . .' '*Morning Echo*, Miss Carlin. Was there a relic? Can you tell us what it was?' 'Say a few words, ladies . . .' 'Here, you've got something heavy in your bag, haven't you, Miss Leame? Let's have a look at it.' More bulbs flashed, a hand reached out, and Nancy cowered back towards the wall of the house. The queen had vanished from her personality and she was like a frightened child or a hunted animal.

'Leave me alone. Don't touch me. Please don't touch me.' She gripped Mary's arm for protection. 'Take me away from here, Miss Carlin. Don't let them pester me any more. Please help me.' Hysteria was clear in her voice as she tried to struggle towards the car park.

'Yes, we'll get away from here.' The public had joined the crowd of journalists now and there was no chance of pushing their way to John and the others. Mary glanced back towards the door and saw that they were completely cut off. The brake was already churning away down the sodden drive, but her car was parked only a few yards to the right of them and the safety of the thing in Nancy's bag seemed to be her own personal charge.

'Come on, let's make a dash for it.' She forced a way through the lines of streaming raincoats and umbrellas and the angry, bitter or pleading faces, and arm in arm the two women ran for the car.

'What is it, Miss Carlin?' They were clear of the grounds when Nancy opened her bag and drew out the little oval object from the vault. 'The metal feels so heavy, almost as if it were solid. And cold too, as cold as ice and sort of clammy.' Under the sodden sky the thing had lost its almost luminous quality and gleamed dully like old pewter.

'Do you still believe it may be the relic, Miss Carlin? Even though Railstone lied, though he was mad when he said he would not die, do you think this may be a holy thing?'

'I believe in the possibility.' The orb kept drawing Mary's eyes towards it and she had to force herself to watch the road which was almost hidden by a solid sheet of water. 'But a lot of research will be done, and even then we may never know the truth, Miss Leame.'

'Nancy, please call me Nancy, my dear. We're friends now. Good friends, Mary. But don't let's go back to Marne and the others. There will be more reporters at Marne's house and I can't stand being questioned. They'll open that chest and prove that he was just a poor maniac. Everybody will laugh at me again.' She turned and looked back towards the Hall, just visible as the car climbed out of the valley.

'What a shame it all is, Mary. Mother always said that there was a family estate, but she never told me where it was. And now that I've found the place they are going to bury it under water.

'Please let's go somewhere where we can talk, Mary; just you and I; only for a few minutes. I can't bear the thought of their faces when they open the chest and find nothing but worthless rubbish and the proof that Martin Railstone was a poor lunatic. Please, Mary. We can study the thing together and show them that it is the relic. We're friends and we can stop them laughing at us.'

* * *

The minutes had dragged out into hours and now Mary sat alone in the sitting-room of her bungalow with the orb on the desk before her and the sound of Nancy's breathing drifting in from the bedroom across the hall.

Because of the rain they had not been able to find a café that was open and it was in a public house that Nancy had poured out her miseries and dreams and ambitions. She had told Mary about the drabness of her life before Buller came on the scene and broke the news of her inheritance. The lack of friends, the jobs she could never hold down, the constant visits to doctors and hospitals and mental institutions, and the weekly pocket money doled out by Mrs Atkins. Excitement about material gains had been her first reaction to Buller's promises. Money to buy clothes and holidays and a house in the country. Power to win friends and admirers and make her a somebody at last.

But that had been the small beginning to her dreams. Once Marne had shown her pictures of Railstone and proved her resemblance to him, after he had told her of Railstone's great powers, after she had tried to read his verse, only understanding enough to excite her, the material gains became quite unimportant. Fantasy and the ability to daydream may be excellent things when under control, but they had completely taken over Nancy's mind. At the moment when she had stepped into the inner vault, she had honestly believed that supernatural forces were at work and that the body of her long-dead ancestor would awaken at her kiss.

All this she told Mary, drinking bottle after bottle of strong 'Export Ale' while the rain poured down the windows of the bar and the cup, or orb, or whatever the object was, gleamed on the bench beside them. Railstone had not awakened, he had let her down, but the possession of the thing made her still feel like a priestess. The relic was her only interest now, and over and over again she made Mary repeat the legends of the Grail: how Joseph had held the vessel beneath the Cross and brought it to Britain, the mystical powers attached to it, and the knights' endless quest.

The time was well after seven when at last Mary persuaded her that the chest might not contain mere rubbish but proof of Railstone's continued genius, and that they should go and see what Marne and the others had discovered. But that was not to be. By the door of the pub Nancy had suddenly stumbled and leaned heavily against the wall to support herself. Her dark face looked much paler and there were beads of sweat on her forehead.

'Sorry, Mary, so very sorry, but I can't go there. I still can't face them.' Her voice wheezed like a broken-winded dray-horse on a hill. 'Must sleep for a little while. Must lie down.'

'What is it, Nancy? Are you ill?' Mary had tried to dissuade her from drinking so quickly, but she had had five bottles of the strong beer. 'How do you feel?'

'Hot and then cold and terribly, terribly tired.' Nancy staggered to the doorway and held out her hands into the rain to moisten her face. 'I felt like that in the vaults too. Cold in the first room and then warm in the second. When I put my cheek against his poor dead face it seemed as if something was – was burning my skin.' She had walked uncertainly to the car and almost fallen into the seat.

'We're not only friends, Mary, but partners now. The relic belongs to you as well as me, because you're the first real friend I've ever had in my life, apart from Ethel who is so old and dull.

'I don't want to be a nuisance, Mary, but could we go to your house so that I can rest for a bit? If you haven't a spare bedroom it doesn't matter. A divan, a sofa, a mattress on the floor will do, but I must lie down.' She had not spoken another word during the journey to the bungalow, and leaned heavily on Mary's shoulder as she helped her inside and put her to bed.

Surely it was only the drink that had affected her. Mary got up and peered into the bedroom. Nancy lay between the sheets wearing Mary's dressing-gown and a pair of her pyjamas; once again she considered fetching a doctor, and then dismissed the idea. Nancy was sleeping heavily but quite peacefully and though her face looked slightly swollen, she was not hot enough to have a high fever. Five bottles of strong beer was a great deal for somebody unused to alcohol and there was nothing to worry about, though in the morning Nancy would feel very sorry for herself. Leaving the door ajar, Mary returned to the sitting-room and sat down facing the relic again.

What a curious thing it was. An oval vessel, slightly larger than a cricket ball, with a round belly and a flanged base which suggested that it might have been attached to another object. There were flanges just inside the lip as well, showing that it must once have had a stopper and, below the lip, a series of small but deeply carved symbols which might be hieroglyphics. Acting as a lower margin to the symbols was a line of 'S' shapes and beneath them a number of inverted Tau crosses. The craftsmanship looked more Greek or Egyptian than Hebrew and surely it was a curious vessel to have been found at the inn in Jerusalem. Still, Mary was no expert on the period and she intended to ask a friend at the British Museum to examine it in the morning. She raised the thing for a moment, again struck by the weight and clammy coldness of the metal, and glanced nervously towards the window, feeling intense irritation towards Nancy Leame. The relic should have been locked up in a bank safe, not left lying exposed with one woman to guard it.

Assuming that it was the relic, of course. When she had first seen the object in the tomb her hopes had soared, and in the car and in the public house they had been only slightly deflated. But now, with the thing on the desk before her and an Anglepoise lamp lighting up its details clearly, Mary's doubts were increasing.

In the first place, it might have been used as a cup, but hardly designed as one. While the base and belly were broad and made her think of a stemless brandy glass, the mouth was too small to be drunk from with any comfort. Secondly, though the outside appeared archaic enough, apart from its high, polished shine, the interior looked almost modern. Mary had slight engineering knowledge, but she fancied that the metal must have been machined to produce so smooth a surface. And that was clearly impossible.

Or was it? Martin Railstone had been a talented engineer. Was she looking at another of his bitter jokes? A hoax to mock the devout who finally found it? As Mary considered that possibility, a lorry thundered up the street outside, its broken exhaust bellowing like laughter. She got up to close the window and draw the curtains, and then changed her mind. The house opposite belonged to the cathedral choir school and was used as a holiday annexe for boys whose parents were abroad or could not have them at home for one reason or another. Her friend Mike Jackson, the second music master, was in charge at the moment and was busily rehearsing his 'Tudor Miscellany' for the autumn concert. Through the pounding rain the melody of 'Greensleeves' came clear and pure and oddly comforting. She went out into the hall and listened at the bedroom door. Nancy sounded as if she were still sleeping peacefully, and she returned to her desk with at least that worry out of her mind.

But what could the thing be? One medieval account described it as an orb, another as a drinking vessel, and the grave-robber had said that it was a box or container and very heavy. That was certainly true; also there was something vaguely unpleasant about the cold, clammy feel of the metal. As she fingered the object, turning it round on the desk, she suddenly noticed that the polished belly was also engraved with finely traced lines which she had not noticed before. Three of them formed a hypotenuse triangle, while the others appeared to make up squares, though they were too faint to see clearly. She held a magnifying glass over the pattern and gave a little gasp of astonishment.

'The sum of the square of the hypotenuse is equal to the sum of the square of the other two sides.' Quite automatically and out of the blue the formula came to her and she whispered the words aloud.

Why on earth should anybody have engraved Pythagoras's theorem on the object? Certainly not merely as a decoration. It might be a law of nature, but had small artistic merits. To show that its maker had been a man of learning who knew the unbreakable canons of the universe? Possibly, and that appeared to rule out Martin Railstone. If he had wished to air his learning he would have chosen something much less obvious. To Railstone the Pythagorean triangle would have seemed as common a piece of knowledge as the two-times table.

But – yes, there was a second geometric design on the other side as well; a series of arcs. Mary couldn't remember what theorem they demonstrated, but it had something to do with the radius of a circle.

Who had placed them there? For what possible reason had the vessel been so curiously decorated? Why did they appear to tell her that it was no Christian relic, but a symbol of cruelty and menace? Why did they suggest that the person who had fashioned them had done so for a very sinister purpose? She lowered the glass, turned nervously towards the window and asked herself a personal question. 'You are a grown woman, you have been given an expensive education; how can you be frightened of a little, empty, lifeless container that can harm nobody?'

Across the street the boys were singing a gay madrigal, the room was warm and cosy, so why did she feel exactly the same as she had done in her aunts' rat-infested house or when she had followed Norseman down the corridors of Caswell Hall? Why should she sense that something cunning and hostile and completely merciless was watching her?

Fourteen

'I've waited a long time for this, Wilde.' Lord Marne watched the heavy chest being manhandled into the room. The furniture had been pulled back against the walls, and the bearers lowered their burden on to the centre of the carpet.

'What's your guess? Are we going to find evidence of great genius or mere senility and mania?' The tension had clearly distressed Marne, for his voice had lost its usual confidence, and John suspected he was talking to control his impatience. Long ago Norseman had considered that he looked like a professional pugilist. He still did, but one who had taken terrible punishment at the ropes.

'Have all our efforts and everything that has happened been worthwhile, or was the man insane and have I been following a meaningless illusion?'

'I'm not very good at guessing, Lord Marne, but you'll know very soon.' John saw Blondin open a tool kit and select two long chrome-steel chisels. He was almost as curious as Marne and the others to know what the chest contained; already his fingers itched for a typewriter, but he was extremely worried about the way Mary and Nancy Leame had gone off, taking the vessel with them. There were a lot of unscrupulous people about and if the thing was what Mary claimed, it would be worth a king's ransom. Also, Nancy had a long record of mental illness, and the sudden sense of power and possession might have aggravated her condition.

Still, Mary was a sensible girl and she could look after herself. John glanced at his companions. Erich Beck appeared to have forgotten his fears of bacteriological danger and was lighting his pipe. But Marjorie Wooderson was staring at the chest with much the same expression of awe that Mary had given to the relic, while even the cynical Sir Gordon Lampton appeared boyishly eager. The lid of the chest bore the Railstone crest; a falcon and a crouching cat, and below the crest had been carved the motto of Henry the Navigator: 'To live is not necessary – to discover is necessary.' A strange maxim for Railstone, he thought. The man had lived to a great age and had been completely careless of the lives of others. He had considered that his very touch was death to his fellows, but that he himself might be immortal. Would there be another booby trap behind that lid, John wondered. Would a second bronze missile rear up when the catches were released?

'See that you fix 'em on good and tight, Linda.' Blondin had inserted the chisels behind the tongues of the locks and the woman was fitting two tubular bars over the handles.

'Good. You'd better all stand back a bit, though I'm not expectin' any fun and games. If there is a booby trap, it's bound to be spring-loaded and the springs would have lost their tension donkey's years ago. But I once read a story of Conan Doyle's about a box like this. Can't remember the title or exactly what happened, but something pretty nasty came out of it. Right, Len, 'ere goes, and bloody gently does it.' Keeping well away from the sides of the chest, Blondin and his henchman bore down on the levers.

'Thank you, Blondin. You have done very well indeed.' Marne waited for the men to remove their tools. The complete anti-climax had come as a surprise to everybody. John, for instance, had half expected an explosion, or another spike to fly out, or even some toad-like creature from the pages of M. R. James to make an appearance. But once the chisels had gained a fulcrum the old brass catches had offered the slightest resistance, and Blondin had raised the lid with scarcely a creak of protest. The chest was open, though whatever it contained was hidden by a length of faded velvet bearing the same crest and motto as the lid.

' "To live is not necessary – to discover is necessary." Till only recently I believed that myself.' Erich Beck took a pace forward and stared down at the cloth. Though the room was cool, there was a hint of moisture on his forehead, looking quite out of place on the slightly wrinkled skin, as if a lizard were sweating. 'But now I am wondering whether to live is not the most important thing we can do.'

'No, Professor, as Miss Leame is not here, I think it is my right to remove the covering.' Beck was reaching towards the velvet but Marne pushed him gently aside. He looked both excited and exhausted as he went down on his knees, and his hand trembled as it drew aside the cloth.

The velvet was not the final covering, though there was no anti-climax about the thing behind it: a panel of painted wood; and even John, who had not been impressed by Railstone's earlier paintings, realized that he was looking at something quite extraordinary. The picture was partly a self-portrait, and the date showed that it had been executed three years before the artist's death. Railstone's face filled the whole panel, and it was not merely a man's face, but a landscape. The eyes were a pale sun and a moon, the hair gave the effect of immensely high and distant mountains, while the blue cheeks and the wrinkles and the clefts of the chin were seas and rivers and lakes. Shadows across the forehead depicted a group of kneeling figures and they were all staring up at a replica of the little silver-coloured object that Nancy had lifted from the floor of the tomb. The object had been painted to suggest violent motion and the shadowy figures of its watchers hinted at sadness and despair; disillusioned crusaders who must fight on, but know that the quest will always end in failure. All this Martin Railstone had shown with a few deft strokes of the brush, and each of his audience knew that they were looking at a product of complete insanity or great genius.

'I've no idea what it represents, Desmond; a treatment of the Grail legend, perhaps. But I do know that it is a masterpiece.' Marjorie Wooderson bent over Marne's shoulder. 'Even if we find nothing else, this makes everything worth while.'

'There will be more, much more.' Marne's voice was faint against the drumming of the rain on the windows. Inch by inch, foot by foot, water would be filling the valley, rivulets pouring down the hillsides, the river swelling back against the barrier of the dam, and the lake and the moat overflowing. Soon Railstone's house and his body would be buried, but the strangeness of his painting held them all rapt.

'I know that this is just the doorway to the treasure house.' Marne's fingers were crooked like talons as he removed the picture and handed it to her, revealing another panel of plain wood with a large calf-bound volume lying on top of it. With extreme slowness he pulled himself to his feet and carried the book across to a table. John knew that Marne was only fifty-five, but he moved like a very old man and his hands were shaking so badly that he could hardly fit his spectacles into position.

'I don't understand.' He frowned as he opened the book and his voice was weak and quavering. The pages were covered with tiny scribbled symbols which might be some form of sign writing or hieroglyphics, but appeared as meaningless as the doodlings on a telephone directory. 'He was insane then. This tells us nothing.' Marne's fingers flicked clumsily through the pages and it became clear that the whole volume was filled with the same apparently meaningless scribbles.

'Look for yourself, Marjorie.' He pushed it towards her and stood by the table breathing heavily.

'But I saw some writing on the cover.' Mrs Wooderson glanced at the open pages and then closed the book to show that a sheet of parchment had been pasted on to the leather board. She leaned forward and started to read aloud.

'"In this volume I have placed all that I have done and all that has been revealed to me. This is the record of my life on earth and also in eternity."' John stifled an irreverent smile, suddenly imagining that a television announcer had proclaimed 'Martin Railstone, this is your life' before an applauding audience.

'"This book and a few poor pictures which will be found in the chest were executed by a man's hand, but it was not a man's mind that guided that hand. If you are she destined to receive my legacy, receive also my blessing and the gift of patience. Put down the book, close the chest and lay your face against mine, my dear one."' The paper was badly stained, the writing cramped, and Mrs Wooderson read slowly, enunciating each word as if it were holy writ.

'"Then wait in patience as I did after I had deciphered the symbols and released the stopper. But do not share my fears that came after the holy thing lay open before my eyes. The terror that followed when I had incised my arm, emptied the vessel and allowed every grain of its precious contents to unite with my body."'

'Cor, you've gotta hand it to him.' Blondin gave a mock shudder. 'Just imagine the old party doing that, and 'im thinking it was the Grail. Must 'ave took a lot of guts.'

'"Soon – very soon the power will come to you as it did to me and you will understand what you have inherited."' Mrs Wooderson had raised her voice at the interruption. '"I have yet many things to say unto you, but you cannot bear them now."'

'That's odd.' Lampton lifted his eyebrows. 'The man was dotty of course, but why should he quote Saint John's gospel? – Are you feeling all right, Lord Marne?' His cynicism had changed to concern, because Marne really did look ill and there was a fleck of froth on his lower lip.

'No, I'm not well, but let me read, Marjorie. I think I know what he will have written next.' Marne staggered as he took the book from her and John saw that the froth was turning pink.

'"If you are not she for whom I have been waiting, you will

understand nothing, and I curse you. If you have presumed to touch my body, then I pity you, because you, my friend, are very close to death." ' As if obeying an order, Marne's mouth opened wide, blood gushed over the faded parchment, and he toppled forward. He was dead before he reached the floor.

★　　★　　★

'Apart from Nancy Leame who is asleep, you are quite alone in the house, nobody is watching you and there is nothing to be frightened of. So stop being a superstitious little fool and pull yourself together.' Mary spoke aloud for reassurance, but the feeling that she was being watched remained.

Was the smell merely imaginary too? She had noticed it when she went out into the hall a few minutes ago. A thick cloying odour rather like garlic; pungent though not unpleasant. Perhaps she had left the gas on when she made Nancy's coffee and a saucepan was burning. Mary went into the kitchen, but the smell was much fainter there and the sight of unlit gas burners, shining tiles and gay crockery did give her some slight reassurance. Whatever it was, the odour must have come in from outside; possibly fumes from the lorry with the leaking exhaust.

She returned to the desk and picked up the magnifying glass, noticing another feature of the vessel which the naked eye had missed. The 'S' shapes beneath the hieroglyphics, if that was what they were, did not consist of separate symbols, but were lightly joined together except at one point, and they diminished in size from left to right. She twisted the vessel anticlockwise and the clear effect of a segmented serpent in motion hinted at their probable purpose. If the hieroglyphics consisted of instructions to release some locking device, did the serpent's direction show how the stopper must be turned from its flanges? According to tradition, Joseph of Arimathaea had placed his Master's blood in a simple cup taken from the inn, but this object was sophisticated and had obviously been designed as a sealed container. The thing also contained a puzzle, the secrets of which could only be discovered by an intelligent being. Had the geometric symbols been put there to arouse that being's curiosity and prompt him to study the hieroglyphics?

'A is Eve's apple, so tempting, so red.
A is for Anne, lovely Anne whom I wed.'

The boys were singing one of Mike Jackson's *Variations on Nursery Rhymes* now. He had played it to her last term and, though she had enjoyed the melody, the theme of the old king, dying and haunted by his past cruelties, had saddened her.

'B is for Boleyn, so fair on my bed.
C is the chopper that chopped off her head.'

Yes, very sad, but why should she find it sickening? Why should the very sight and feel of a small metal object frighten her? How had the memories of her aunts' house and the long corridors of Caswell Hall invaded the bungalow?

'Little Boy Blue, come blow your horn . . .'

The tune came tripping through the window, light and airy as if it were mocking her, and she recalled how Martin Railstone's dead face had seemed to leer and smile from its slab.

'The Sheep's in the meadow, the Cow's in the corn.'

It was at that moment that Mary realized that her fears were not imaginary and that she was not alone in the room. Something really was watching her and she could see it and smell it and hear it. A tiny reflection on the surface of the orb; the cloying odour growing much stronger; a soft scraping sound as if something heavy and decayed was being dragged over the carpet.

'But where is the Man who looks after the Sheep?'

The melody lilted on, but to Mary the world contained nothing except the reflection on the metal, the thick cloying odour and the sound of a heavy body shuffling across the floor till it stopped behind her chair. She forced herself to turn and look down.

'It's you, only you.' She gasped with relief, seeing the bedroom slippers she had lent to Nancy, a pair of her own pyjamas, the hem of her dressing-gown. 'You must be feeling better, Nancy. I'm so glad, but what a shock you gave me.'

'Little Boy Blue he is fast asleep.'

But he was not asleep. The song ended, Mary smiled up at the face above the dressing-gown and then stopped smiling. During the few seconds she remained conscious, she just screamed, screamed, screamed.

Fifteen

JOHN drove Marne's shooting brake as fast as he possibly could, but the wipers were almost useless against the volume of the rain, and the windscreen was obscured by water. On the seat beside him, Erich Beck sat bolt upright, with a gloved hand gripping the arm rest. He no longer looked gnome-like, but hard and purposeful; a Prussian general throwing in his last reserves.

'Do not touch him, any of you.' Beck had forced them back when Marne crumpled on the carpet, and pulled on the gloves before kneeling down beside the body, feeling for pulse and heart as he had done when George Banks died.

'Well, Sir Gordon,' he said finally, releasing the dead wrist. 'Did Marne suffer from Rheinfelder's syndrome too, or was Martin Railstone telling the truth? Could his touch kill? Did it remain lethal after two hundred years?'

'I refuse to believe that. Please ring for an ambulance, Mrs Wooderson.' Lampton stuttered slightly and his face was drawn with shock and bewilderment. 'There must be a rational explanation, Professor, there has to be. We know nothing of Marne's medical history. There may have been some vascular weakness.

After all, he was not a young man and opening that chest had become his obsession. If there were a heart condition, the excitement could have been too much for him.'

'I hope you are right, sir.' As the German stood up, John was struck by the bleakness of his expression; the mask of a man who has seen extreme evil and wishes to hide personal emotion.

'All the same, Banks said that he touched something warm in the vault and he and Marne both died in the same way. That is a fact. It is also a fact that Railstone prophesied that only one person could touch his body and not die. Remember that neither of them suffered from dropsy, that their hair was not red and they were not related to the Railstone family. No, don't go near him, Sir Gordon.' He held out his arm. 'Most probably the organism will have degenerated after failing to unite with its host, but there is no point in taking risks.'

'Professor Beck, though I respect your reputation, this is nonsensical.' The shock was wearing off and Lampton had regained some of his urbanity. 'Are you seriously suggesting that Railstone was the carrier of some contagious illness harmless to himself but lethal to everybody else? That after his death the spores of the organism remained dormant in the corpse for two hundred years? That the warmth and moisture of Marne's hand reactivated the spores and they penetrated the skin . . . ?' He broke off and shrugged, completely at a loss to consider such an absurdity. 'No, sir, there must be a much more rational explanation for what happened.'

'Again I hope you are right.' Beck turned to Mrs Wooderson, who had finished her telephone call. 'Madam, you were a close friend of Marne's, I believe. Do you happen to know whether he kept any firearms in the house; a revolver, perhaps? Yes, I may be mad. I have no licence, nor do I know against whom or what I may need to use a gun, but if there is one in the house, please, please find it for me.' He pleaded at the astonishment on their faces.

'In a way I hope I am mad. All the same, I would ask you to remember the last line of the inscription on the slab: "Dove è la Donna che Mi può dare la Vita."'

'Thank you.' Marjorie Wooderson had reluctantly produced an

automatic from the drawer of a desk and Beck checked the clip
before stuffing it into his pocket. 'Well, where is she, Mr Wilde?
Lord Marne was not the only person who touched that corpse.
I think we should go and look for her. If I am right, your Miss
Carlin may be in very grave . . .' Beck never finished the sentence,
because John was already hurrying out of the room and, with a
final glance at Marne's lifeless body, Beck followed him. Now he
sat stiffly on the car seat, his eyes flickering from the speedometer
to the dashboard clock and the fingers of his left hand playing with
the automatic, as if the feel of it gave him comfort.

'Railstone knew what he was talking about, Mr Wilde. He had
a very good reason for describing his heiress so exactly, but I have
neither the time nor the inclination to discuss it with you now.' He
spoke like a lecturer who is bored by an importunate student.

'But at least tell me how you can be so sure.' The tyres skidded
against the kerb as John swung the car around a bend. They were
travelling at over fifty with visibility almost down to zero, and
there was no knowing where Mary and Nancy had gone, though
the bungalow seemed the best bet. John had accepted Beck's word
that Mary might be in danger, but he still didn't understand why.
Nancy had laid her face against Railstone's, she might be ill or dead
already, but why should Mary be affected? After all, several people
had touched George Banks's body and received no ill effects.

'I am only sure on two points, Mr Wilde. Martin Railstone was
correct in saying that his body was a lethal weapon and the condition was not produced by any Christian relic.' Beck's face looked
white and fungoid in the glare of approaching headlights.

'However much Sir Gordon may sneer at my anxieties, I do
regard myself as the only expert on the subject.'

'An expert? How on earth can you say that?' John was completely blinded by the lights and the streaming windscreen, and he
braked till the car had passed them. 'It is only a matter of weeks
since Banks died and you've had no time or opportunity to study
the thing that killed him.'

'Quite correct, Mr Wilde, but Banks and Marne may not have
been isolated cases, you see, and Miss Carlin's relic could have had
a double.' Beck gripped the seat still tighter as John accelerated

around another bend, then again his bleak smile flitted from John's face to the dashboard clock and finally to the gun.

' "Into whatsoever house I enter, it shall be for the benefit of the sick." That was the oath I took when I was a young man: how terribly I betrayed its code.' He closed his eyes and did not speak again till the car drew up before the bungalow.

There was a light on in the hall: everything must be all right. Mary and Nancy Leame were there and they would get a shock at this unexpected arrival. John forced himself to believe that as he switched off the engine. Sir Gordon Lampton was correct in thinking Beck was deranged and that some perfectly normal illness had killed Marne and Banks. Mary was in no danger and in a moment she would tell him so herself.

'Wait, Mr Wilde. It is better that I go first.' Beck barked like a drill sergeant as John started to hurry forward, then lifted a medical bag from the floor of the car and strode purposefully up the path with the automatic in one hand and the bag in the other; shoulders back and chest stuck out, as if on his way to a parade.

There was nothing to worry about, because everything that had happened before had been to do with darkness and decay; the welcoming lights reassured John at each step. He remembered smelling the stench of damp and woodrot while Norseman's body hung suspended in the gloom. Surely evil could find no resting place in this modern, brightly lit bungalow? Lampton was right and the pistol in Beck's hand was just another sign of the mania which Railstone's story seemed to inspire.

'They did not lock the door.' The German kicked it open in the best motion-picture manner and they stepped inside.

'Miss Carlin, are you there?' He had relaxed slightly at the sight of the tidy hallway with the prints on the walls, gay dust-jackets in a bookcase and a bowl of flowers. 'Can you hear me, Miss Carlin?'

'Mary, where are you?' Even as he added his voice to Beck's, John's reassurance started to drain away. It was because of the smell at first; a cloying, pungent, though not really unpleasant odour which seemed to be seeping up from the floor. Then he saw that the mirror beside the sitting-room door had been broken and a gob of reddish liquid was congealing on the shattered glass.

Finally Mary's voice from behind a second door which led to the kitchen told him that something was horribly wrong.

'John, John darling. You must go away. You must, must get away from here.' Every word hinted at hysteria. 'She won't hurt me, but you must leave at once.' John rushed at the door, but Beck reached it first, dropping the bag and pushing the gun into his pocket. His gloved hands turned the key and the handle in one movement, but he opened the door very, very slowly. So slowly that John pulled him aside and pushed past him into the kitchen.

'It's all right, darling. There's nothing to worry about, Mary.' She lay crouched beside the kitchen table like a sick animal and she whimpered while he lifted her to her feet. Her face was blotched with tears and her whole body shuddered in his arms.

'Must get out, John. Must get away and quickly. You and Beck first. She won't hurt me. That was promised.' She stood staring across the hall towards the door of the sitting room. 'Go now, while you can.'

'Listen to me, Miss Carlin.' Beck reached out and tilted her face towards his own. 'You are in a state of shock, so pull yourself together. Where is Miss Leame? What happened to her?'

'Miss Leame, Nancy Leame.' Mary laughed hysterically. 'Nancy doesn't exist any more, though she kept saying she was my friend – that she wouldn't hurt me. Try and understand, both of you. Nancy has changed – altered. I saw her before I fainted, I heard her voice talking to me when I came round. She locked me in, so that she wouldn't hurt me. Oh, my God – the sight of her – the way she sounded.'

'Where is she, Miss Carlin? Where did she go? It is essential that you tell me that.' Beck slapped her face lightly but there was no need for him to wait for Mary's answer. From across the hall came the crash of breaking glass and rending metal followed by a deep gurgling, chuckling sound which made John think of some reptilian creature crawling out of a deep hole in the earth.

'Don't go in there! For God's sake, let's get out while we can!' Mary was screaming and struggling against John's grip, but Beck had already walked across the hall. The door was locked with the key on the inside, and beyond it the sounds were repeated and

there came a second crash of glass. He placed the muzzle of the
pistol very carefully against the lock and fired three times. The
door swung open with the force of the last explosion and they saw
what had inspired the imagination of Martin Railstone.

Many critics had pondered the nature of the figures in Railstone's 'Dream Landscapes'. Some said that they were part animal,
part human: debased creatures desperately attempting to evolve a
soul. Others considered that the hunched bodies and the hint of
horned skulls suggested that they represented the old gods who
had been driven out by later religions, but who still existed in deso-
late parts of the earth. Still another school stated that they were
not animate at all, but merely vegetation which could take any
form that suited its purpose, like clusters of moss or lichen. In any
event Railstone had depicted the things so vaguely that nobody
could offer a definite opinion.

But John and Mary and Erich Beck saw their model now, though
there was nothing alive in the room. More drops of red liquid
led across the floor to the desk and the little orb, which still lay
beneath the lamp, shining at them like a mocking eye. Behind the
desk, the whole window frame had been torn out and beyond the
gap that glass and steel and timber had once screened, something
was moving: a thing very much like one of Railstone's 'Dream'
figures, which crawled or twisted or writhed away from them to
vanish in the rain.

Sixteen

'I'M NOT suggesting that you've deliberately invented anything,
Miss Carlin, but we've gotta face the facts.' Mr Bob Brown, the
Under Secretary of State for Internal Affairs, had been the leader
of an agricultural trade union before entering Parliament, and he
still looked as if he should be reaping a field. Not with any com-
bine harvester, either, but with a scythe.

'And so far the facts don't add up to much, my girl. It don't
need no lawyer to tell me that.' Mr Brown glared at Mary and
John and Erich Beck in turn. He prided himself on being a bluff,

hearty politician who always spoke his mind, and so far had given an exhibition of domineering rudeness. They were assembled in a room at the Lanchester Police station, Brown having arrived from London less than two hours ago, and he sat at the end of the table with Sir Gordon Lampton and a uniformed superintendent beside him and a nervous secretary hovering at his back. In a wheel-chair by the window lay the gaunt figure of Dr Norseman, who had been allowed out of hospital for the gathering.

'You yourself have admitted that you were scared out of your wits before the woman came into the room and you can't recall exactly what you did see. And you're still scared, aren't you? A baboon could see that much.'

'That's perfectly true, but I've described what I can remember as accurately as possible.' Mary looked away from him and she tried to force her memory back. She could remember the nursery rhyme drifting in through the window, she could remember the cloying odour and the sound of something moving behind her. She could remember the reassuring sight of the bedroom slippers, the pyjamas and the dressing-gown. But some psychological defence mechanism had made the rest vague and shadowy, though she seemed to recall that Nancy's face had been swollen out of all normal proportions, that the flesh was wrinkled like grey furnace slag, and the eyes appeared to be bursting out of their sockets.

What happened afterwards was clear enough, however. She had come to lying on the kitchen floor and heard, first, a slow agonized breathing, then a series of whimpers, then a voice only just recognizable as Nancy's. 'Friends . . . still good friends, Mary. Listen to me, but don't say anything. Don't let me hurt you. Mustn't hurt you, Mary.' Thick and slurred the words had come through the locked door. 'What has happened to me, Mary? Why am I burning? No, don't speak . . . don't make me harm you . . .' There had been the sound of footsteps shuffling away, the crash of breaking glass, a scream and the sound of another door closing. Then silence, till she heard John and Beck shouting her name.

'Quite so, Miss Carlin.' Brown's pencil rapped the table. 'You've certainly given us a bloody lurid description, but I won't go along with its accuracy. Now, let's consider the evidence of you two.' It was the turn of John and Beck to receive his scorn. 'Mr Wilde has described some kind of reptilian creature which he and the Professor both saw. I think we should remember that Mr Wilde is a journalist who has already written a lot of sensational muck about this business. Maybe he hopes that this reptile, or whatever it was, might give him more ammunition for his talents.

'No, just keep quiet, young man. I'm in charge here and don't you forget it.' He had brought his fist crashing down as John started to protest. 'You've told me that you saw the thing and I'm not questioning that you saw something. Nor am I doubting that the window had been torn out by Miss Leame and that would have taken a deal of strength. All the same, I've heard that mental cases are often abnormally strong and, as the super's said, a general call has been put out for her.'

'With respect, Mr Brown, it was not Miss Leame we saw.' John had used all his persuasion to describe that crawling, writhing shape drifting away into the rain and he felt furious at Brown's complete dismissal of his statement. 'The thing we saw was not a woman, not even human.'

'So you've said many times, Mr Wilde. You've also stated that the only lighting in the room came from an Anglepoise lamp over the desk, that the rain outside was torrential, that there was no moon, the nearest street light was a good fifty yards away and you only saw this . . . "creature" was the word you used, for a few brief seconds. It'll take a deal more than that to make me credit your crawling monster, I'm afraid.' He dismissed John with a rap of his pencil and beamed at Gordon Lampton as if welcoming an ally.

'Now, you're the medical expert, Sir Gordon, so let's hear you add the voice of reason to mine. Did your examination of Lord Marne's body show that some biological menace exists, or that dark supernatural forces may be at work, as the Dean appears to believe?'

'The examination of the body suggested several things to me, Mr Brown.' Lampton turned to Beck and gave a brief nod. 'Marne was killed by a series of vascular ruptures caused by an abnormal action of the heart, and he suffered from no longstanding illness which could have accounted for such a condition. I now agree with

Professor Beck that some inorganic substance or micro-organism, which we have so far failed to isolate, was responsible for his death and for the death of George Banks.'

'The devil you do!' Brown scowled as if Lampton had betrayed him personally. 'How can you make such a statement when you don't even know what this substance or bug is?'

'I can only show you what I have seen, Mr Brown.' Sir Gordon got up and walked over to a slide projector which had been placed on another table by the door, and switched it on. To the majority of his audience the photograph it projected on to the opposite wall was meaningless and might have depicted coloured grains of sand or dust spread out on a white surface.

'Even a layman knows that certain plants and animals are able to produce spores as a means of self-preservation, Mr Brown. When placed in conditions where death would normally result, these spores, often needle-sharp, are able to remain alive, though dormant, almost indefinitely. Then, should circumstances alter and become favourable for the organism to thrive – by entering the body of a suitable host, for example – alterations take place in the structure of the spores and the normal life cycle is resumed.' Lampton moved over to the wall and pointed at the lower left-hand corner of the picture.

'This photograph shows a section of Marne's arterial tissue. Even under most intense magnification, the objects are too small for anybody to be certain about their nature, but I believe that they are a minute bacteriological rash of a genus I have never seen or heard of. Where I am pointing there is a suggestion that some of the units have already started to resume their original form. In my opinion there is only one source from which Marne could have been infected in this way.'

'You are honestly suggesting that Marne and Banks died because they touched the body of a man that had been underground for two centuries, Sir Gordon?' Brown gave a snort and smiled triumphantly. 'Then perhaps one of you can tell me why they merely died, but Miss Leame was turned into this crawling horror?' He looked at John with venom, for he was no lover of the *Globe*. After one of his more boorish outbursts, the paper had stated that

Brown's constituents were largely to blame and if people elected hooligans they must expect hooliganism. 'This Frankenstein monster we have heard the representative of the gutter press describe so vividly.'

What exactly had he seen? John ignored the insult and tried to concentrate on remembering. The thing had looked both flat and oval and, though fragments of human clothing had been dragged with it, it was certainly not human and probably not even animal. Brown was correct in saying that his view had been brief and indistinct, but he had had the definite impression that he was not looking at a single individual, but at a mass of amalgamated units which could change their shape and form as the occasion arose.

'I can offer a suggestion, Mr Brown, nothing more.' Sir Gordon turned from the wall and faced him. 'My belief is that Railstone was not merely infected by some disease, but was the carrier of an organism which had somehow become united with his own cellular tissue; much in the way that lichens are separate individuals existing in symbiosis with each other. Marne's system rejected the alien tissue and both host and parasite perished in the ensuing struggle.

'Nancy Leame, however, was a blood relation of Railstone, and she also possessed his physical peculiarities. Surely it is possible that her metabolism might not only accept the invasion, but welcome it?' He returned to the projector and another photograph gleamed on the wall. The slide could have shown a universe, and cells floated like stars and planets and moons; rather beautiful in the purple stain which had been used to reveal their presence. Beside every cell was a tiny, twisted, worm-like shape, some approaching their victims, some encircling them, while others appeared to have entered the human tissue and become united with it.

'That shows a specimen of arterial blood found on the broken mirror in Miss Carlin's bungalow. It certainly came from Nancy Leame, or the thing she had become, and gives us some slight idea of what we may be up against. Here, here and here you can see that human corpuscles and alien cells are existing contentedly in symbiosis.'

'And that's quite enough lecturing from you, Sir Gordon.'

Brown dealt the table another crashing blow with his fist. '"The thing we are up against" indeed. "Existing contentedly."' He had a rough north-country accent, ideally suited to express scorn.

'I'm a patient man, ladies and gentlemen. I came down from London at a moment's notice; I've looked at those trashy paintings and meaningless scribbles taken from Railstone's box, I've listened to Mr Wilde and Miss Carlin describing their X-film horrors and I'm prepared to admit that there is a medical risk involved, though I don't see what's to be done till we find this unfortunate woman. The police are already looking for her: what more do you want, Sir Gordon? Speak up, man, and let's get down to business. I'm a reasonable sort of chap and I'll do anything in my power to help – providing you don't want the Government to declare a Holy War, of course, Dr Norseman.' He glared at the Dean, who was lying back in his wheelchair with his eyes closed and obviously very weak.

'Sir Gordon and Professor Beck have already recommended a course of action, sir.' Brown's secretary was young and ill at ease, and he looked scared out of his wits as he handed his superior a typed sheet of foolscap. 'The measures they suggest are very drastic, and I thought you should hear their explanations before even considering them.'

'Thanks, lad.' Brown put on a pair of spectacles and craned over the paper. He had recently returned from a goodwill visit to the West Indies and his face was deeply tanned. It grew much darker as he read the proposals.

'Glory be to God! Declare a national emergency you say, Sir Gordon. Pump that reservoir full of copper sulphate in case Railstone's corpse has contaminated the water. Evacuate an area twenty miles wide from Lanchester to the bloody coast. Set every research laboratory in the country to work on this bug which you only imagine exists.' He crumpled up the paper and threw it aside like a highly disgusting object.

'Yes, *suggest, think, suspect, imagine*; those are some of the words you've all used in trying to describe it, and now you ask me to do this. Just because two men died of heart failure and one woman is ill, you ask me to recommend this to the Minister. Really, gentlemen, you must be out of your minds. What do you think the Cabinet would say? What do you imagine the P.M. would do? He'd think I was off me ruddy rocker and ask me to resign.'

'You don't understand, do you? You keep talking about a sick woman and you think in terms of disease and normal illness. Don't you realize that we are not in for an epidemic, but an invasion?' Erich Beck had not spoken for the last three-quarters of an hour, but now he had stood up and there was a most curious expression on his face. He looked like a man about to make a decision which he knows will ruin him.

'Miss Leame may no longer exist, you see. Her body may be merely a breeding ground; perhaps the creatures do not need her any more. Perhaps they are already established – multiplying in lakes and rivers, and starting to spread across the whole earth. I know what I am talking about, sir. I am the only person who really does know the threat that hangs over us, and you must do as Sir Gordon says.'

'Then perhaps you'd better sit down and tell us, Professor.' Brown was obviously unsure whether he should be impressed by the outburst or consider Beck insane. 'Come on, out with it.'

The telephone postponed Beck's revelation. It rang shrilly on the table and, with a gesture for him to be silent, the policeman reached out and lifted the receiver.

'Superintendent Jones here. Certainly I'll hold on.' He cupped a hand over the mouthpiece and spoke to Brown.

'When I was informed of this bacteriological menace, I had the so-called relic sent to the Westminster Institute of Metallurgy, sir. Their Director promised to examine it himself and I'm sure he'll put an end to some of Professor Beck's wilder fears.' Jones had an extremely mobile face and it registered his clear belief in Beck's insanity.

'Good afternoon, Dr Cohen. Have you finished your analysis of that singular object so soon then? Ah, that was very good of you.

'What? What's that, Doctor? I know I'm not a scientist, but I thought there was nothing harder than a diamond.' He had been smiling when Cohen came on the line, but he didn't smile now. He appeared completely bewildered, as if unable to believe his own ears.

'Please repeat that, Doctor Cohen. Thank you. Now would you hold the line for just a moment?' He laid down the instrument and looked at Beck with a completely different expression.

'Unless they are incompetent at the Institute, you may have your emergency, Professor. The vessel is cast from an artificial alloy; so hard that a diamond did not even scratch the surface. The molecular structure remained unaltered under intense heat and nuclear radiation, and something called a Haley-Knight Carbon 15 Test failed to produce any reaction.' The projector was still switched on and Jones stared at the wall with its universe of human and alien cells.

'According to Dr Cohen, this suggests that the thing is more than fifteen million years old.'

Seventeen

FOR a time nothing happened. The rain continued, Brown made a grudging report to his superiors, and the police carried on their search for Nancy Leame. No trace of her was found, though fragments of clothing were discovered in a lane some two miles from the bungalow. They were naturally dirty and sodden, but also strangely perforated and crumbling as if moths had been at work in them.

At the British Museum, scholars of several fields studied the orb and the manuscripts found in the chest. Apart from agreeing that the metal had an intense molecular density and was extremely old, they made little of the object itself, while historians and linguists wrangled over the nature of the scribbled signs.

A humble major from the Codes and Cypher Department of the Ministry of Defence finally solved that problem. On a page towards the end of the book, either because he was tired or ill, Railstone had joined two lines of symbols with a short sentence in plain English. In the same way as the Rosetta Stone had provided a key to the hieroglyphics of Ancient Egypt, this gave the major his start. Both cup and manuscript contained complicated sign-writing and their message was a series of promises and threats and orders. But several months passed before this came to light and by then the subject was of purely academic interest, though the major received an O.B.E. for his labours.

In the interests of public order, all newspaper reports were censored and the Ministry of Health issued a mild statement. Three persons had been infected by a so far unidentified virus and two of them had died. The virus was considered to be an abnormal strain of the foot-and-mouth disease which had ravaged the Lanchester district during the previous year and which had somehow become inimical to human beings. There was, however, little cause for further anxiety. The heavy rain would have done a lot to cleanse the ground and Ministry inspectors on the spot considered that the risks of an epidemic were slight. As a purely precautionary measure, schools in the area would remain closed for the time being, and any person suffering from a temperature or a high pulse rate should contact their doctor immediately.

The vast majority of the local inhabitants were unimpressed and they shrugged off that statement as a typical piece of Whitehall interference, if not a deliberate plot to deprive their children of education because of the teacher shortage. Before the month was out three of them ceased to exist, and one survived to tell a very strange story.

A farmer named James Kerr was the first to go: a bitter, sad man who had lost his dairy herd because of the foot-and-mouth outbreak, and who considered the Government had unfairly compensated him. That autumn he had planted winter kale, and told his wife that the flooded fields were the last straw which might ruin them. On the morning when the rain finally stopped, leaving blue skies and the promise of better weather to come, Kerr left the house, taking a dog and a gun with him and saying that he was going to examine the extent of the damage. When the dog returned alone at midday, his wife remembered the gun and her husband's depressed mood and telephoned the police.

Kerr's body was never found, but in the corner of a field lay the gun, his clothing and the contents of his pockets. The clothes were torn, and perforated in the same way as Nancy Leame's, and both barrels of the gun had been fired. The field had been uniformly flattened by the storm, but leading away from Kerr's few remains was a broad swathe which appeared to have been beaten down by something much more solid than rain.

Number two was a postman, Arthur Glossop. He had made his final morning delivery at a lonely house outside the village of Kentham, some nine miles from Lanchester, and the housewife, after reluctantly signing for a registered letter containing a summons for non-payment of rates, had watched him mount his bicycle and peddle away. She was the last person to see him, though Glossop also left his possessions for the police to find. The bicycle and clothing lay at the road-side and the surface of the road looked as though it had recently been swept. Around the bodies of both men and leading away from them were traces of a grey powdery substance, later identified as minute particles of human hair, teeth and nails.

Fred Adams was the name of the man who survived, and he also came from Kentham, to the shame and disgrace of its citizens. Adams lived by casual labour and the good graces of the Ministry of Social Security, and he had spent seven of his twenty-nine years in reform school, prison and mental institution. The charges against him had included petty larceny, breaking and entering, grievous bodily harm and gross indecency. The last had been the most recent, but Adams had not been reformed by his six months in the institution. On the contrary, he had come to glory in his peculiar hobbies and, on the morning in question, was on his way to indulge them further. Why not? he asked himself. If Elsa Wallace was prepared to take her clothes off in Birkdale Spinney, surely he'd be a fool not to take advantage of the fact?

Adams came loping furtively down the road like a straggler fearing ambush, though now and again he looked up at the clear sky with relish. Just the weather for a nice warm sunbath in that clearing in the wood. Before marrying the village schoolmaster Mrs Wallace had been Elsa Gottfried, citizen of Stockholm, and she made a cult of her body. He'd watched her go striding past his mother's cottage only ten minutes ago, and soon she'd be stripped and ready. Adams licked his lips at the prospect of tanned thighs and buttocks and breasts spread out on a plastic sheet above the pine needles for his edification.

'You, Adams, are a contemptible little Peeping Tom and a disgrace to our community.' That was what the magistrate had said, but he didn't think of himself like that at all. 'A compulsive voyeur' was how a psychiatrist at the institution had described his condition and there was a respectable, almost professional, ring to the word; doctor, lawyer, scientist, voyeur. Adams felt proud of his calling, but all the same he ducked quickly over the stile leading to the wood as he heard the sound of Peter Hampton's tractor coming down the lane. Hampton was both a puritan and a brutal drunkard, and he'd threatened to give Adams the hiding of his life if he caught him up to his tricks again. Adams had had a lot of hidings in his time, all of them administered for excellent reasons.

But danger also added spice to his enjoyment, he thought, as he hurried into the wood and the first trees closed around him. To him, each view of naked flesh was a trophy as well as a sexual stimulus, and no scalping Redskin or big-game hunter could have felt more tense excitement than did Fred Adams. The risk of Elsa's screams and recognition, of Hampton's fists and the magistrate's savage sentence merely increased his pleasure and he sidled through the spinney in high heart.

There she was at last, all stark and lovely, just as he knew she would be. He pulled out the binoculars which were his most treasured possession and lowered himself behind the trunk of a tree.

'Cor, what a flamer, what a gift, what a piece of crackling.' Adams chuckled to himself as he studied Mrs Wallace's naked charms. 'Look at them great, gorgeous swingers. She must be bored stiff sleeping with a senile old toad like her husband, God rot the bastard! Probably impotent, I shouldn't wonder.' As a boy he had frequently suffered from the heavy hand of the headmaster, and this view of his wife stretched out bare and luscious in the sunlit clearing was like a personal triumph that paid off a lot of old scores.

What a mean swine Hampton was to use fuel like that. The tractor must have turned up the lane at the other side of the spinney and its fumes were drifting towards him on the slight breeze, thick and cloying and pungent. Real rot-gut he was burning to make such a stench, and even the birds disliked it. Adams started as a cock pheasant rocketed past him in a blaze of colour, a jay screamed and two wood-pigeons fluttered overhead.

Damn Hampton! That rotten fuel was going to stop the show. Through the glasses he could see a frown of distaste on the woman's face and she stood up, giving him a fine view, but he realized it was going to be the last. Already she was reaching for her clothes, and he couldn't blame her with that stink spoiling everything.

That was strange. The smell was strong, so why couldn't he hear the tractor, and what was the noise that he could hear? A soft, rustling sound as if grass and pine needles were moving in a gale. There was only a light breeze blowing, so why should that ridge of bracken beyond the clearing sway and ripple as it did?

Christ! She must have seen him. Beneath the rustling noise and the raucous cries of a second pheasant, Adams distinctly heard a human scream and he lowered the binoculars and drew back still further behind the tree trunk. 'Medical report or no medical report, if you appear before us again, you will go to prison for a very long time,' the magistrate had promised, and he knew him to be a man of his word. He'd better get out quick and just hope that she hadn't recognized him.

It was all right, though. Elsa screamed again, and he saw that she wasn't looking at him. Her back was turned and she stood rigid on the sheet, staring at the bracken as if unable to move. But from the bracken something was moving towards her.

'Like a bloody great carpet being dragged forward,' was the way Adams later described what he saw, though he didn't stay long enough to get a good view. He ran for his life, leaving his precious binoculars behind him, but just before he ran he did see enough to realize that the carpet was either a liquid or composed of millions of tiny particles. It lapped around Elsa Wallace's feet, caressed her ankles and then trickled up over her knees and thighs and started to pull her down towards it.

Eighteen

ADAMS could have kept quiet. As he ran staggering out of the wood, he realized that if he reported what he had seen he might easily end up before the magistrates again. But the horror of that obscene carpet rearing up over the bracken and lapping around Elsa's body was far stronger than his fears of prison, and he went to the police. Complete disbelief of his story was the first reaction, then anxiety when the mangled shreds of the woman's clothing were discovered, finally local panic. Because during the following day three more victims were claimed by *Nuber Caswellensis*, the *Caswell Cloud* as it later became known.

A child playing on a pavement was the first of them and she vanished in broad daylight with several reliable witnesses to testify to what happened to her. She had been sitting cross-legged with a doll on her lap when the sound came. A rumbling, belching gurgle, deep and loud, from the grating of a rain-water drain, followed by an odour that reminded the witnesses of burning garlic. Then, up through the grating had come something resembling a gout of soot. It had screened the child's body for an instant and then drawn back the way it had come. When the air cleared there was nothing on the pavement except grey powder, clothes, and the child's doll. The village from which the little girl vanished was seven miles from Lanchester and the time was shortly after nine o'clock in the morning. Before noon she was to have companions.

Because the grating was intact there was no question of the child being alive, and all that could be done was to destroy the thing that had killed her. A solution of copper sulphate, strong enough to wipe out any known animal or vegetable life, was pumped into the drain, which was then flushed out by the fire brigade. When considered completely safe, two sewer men entered the drain to make an inspection. They did not return and, so far, nobody had volunteered to go down and look for them.

After that there could be no more bland reassurances from the

Ministry, no more muzzling the press and radio and television sta-
tions. An area twenty miles wide and stretching from Lanchester
to the coast would have to be evacuated as Sir Gordon Lampton
had demanded, and the military would join with the medical services to eradicate the menace. From every newspaper and radio
receiver and television screen the experts gave their views and
most of them attempted to offer comfort.

Where had the thing come from? There was no answer to that,
though the structure of the metal orb suggested several interesting
possibilities.

If such theories were incorrect, and the organism had an extra-
terrestrial origin, how did it function? Had the vessel contained
spores, as Sir Gordon believed, which had become reactivated
when Railstone opened the vessel in the first place? Had they
coexisted in his body, the alien unit joining with the human cells,
and then lain dormant at his death – till another host with similar
physical characteristics appeared?

Above all, what had happened to Nancy Leame? Had *Nuber
Caswellensis* reached a debased form in Railstone's body and did it
require more than human cells to support it? Was the secret to be
found in the female hormone system, perhaps? Had Nancy Leame
been used as a breeding ground, and were the creatures now capa-
ble of spreading their own cells far and wide?

What actual form did the thing or things now take, and what
must be done to destroy them, or render them harmless? In the
Dean's study, the face of Lord Bulman of Bolton, Master of a
Cambridge college, frowned from the television screen.

That was, of course, a difficult question to answer at this stage,
but every course of action was being considered and medical science would soon come up with an answer, Bulman assured his
audience.

The important thing was to put matters in their true perspective.
Some uninformed persons had spoken of a hostile group intelligence – a mass of tiny beings working purposefully together in
the way that ants and bees are supposed to do. That was of course
absurd, though it was true to say that the human brain itself was
merely a vast network of individual cells and electrical impulses.

As to the physical form, there was not enough evidence to arrive at any definite conclusion, though eye-witnesses had described something resembling a carpet of dust or liquid moving across the ground. The complete disappearance of the victims with the exception of the powdery substance composed of hair, nail and other particles, suggested that the organism was able to absorb all human cell tissue with the exception of secreted matter.

Lord Bulman closed on a note of cheer. Though he agreed that the authorities were right in ordering the evacuation of the area, there was no need to panic and all would be well, provided the public kept calm. In days . . . no, more likely in hours or even minutes, he was convinced that his colleagues would come up with a solution and the scourge would be wiped from the face of the earth.

'Heard enough?' Norseman glanced at his companions, John and Mary and Beck, and then switched off the receiver and pulled back the curtains. What should have been a quiet evening in the little cathedral town resembled the height of the London rush hour. Buses and lorries, private cars and taxis, motor bicycles and mopeds and push-bikes were all moving slowly up the street that led to the London road, and a queue of pedestrians stretched the full half-mile from the cathedral to the railway station. There was no sign of panic yet, the police obviously had matters well in hand, but everybody was getting away from the thing that Lord Bulman intended to wipe out in so short a time.

A rattling, hammering roar masked the drone of the traffic crawling out of Lanchester, and the Dean watched two helicopters circle the cathedral and swing away towards the open country to the south and west. Surely the organism must be destroyed by now, he thought. Since dawn aircraft had been spraying the fields and woodlands and dumping chemicals. Every lake and stream and river had been dyed blue by copper sulphate and their surfaces were foul with dead fish and reptiles. A belch of soot, carpets of dust apparently driven by the wind when no wind blew, clear liquid oozing along the ground like oil: that was how eye-witnesses had described the phenomenon. A mass of minute particles hidden by vegetation, moving under water, concealed by gravel or mud, quite invisible till the time came for it to strike.

'The poison must have worked by now. Those boys will put paid to the brutes, if they haven't done so already.' Norseman turned from the helicopters and smiled at his guests. Though still very weak he tried to appear strong and self-confident. 'Within a few hours the danger will be over.'

'Do you think so, Mr Dean?' Erich Beck was standing by a map of the district spread out on a table. 'I wish that you were right, but I know what we are up against. There was once a method to destroy those brutes, as you call them, but we today lack the means. While we stand here their organisms are not merely becoming physically stronger but gaining in intelligence too.'

'You mean a group intelligence that Lord Bulman dismissed?' Mary looked across at him, but in her mind's eye she could see the series of paintings taken from Railstone's chest and the story that they told: of a world that was dying, and of the longing of its inhabitants to perpetuate their race. They must have known that there could be no actual survival, but had the sporified elements of their cellular tissue been their hope for immortality? Had hundreds, perhaps thousands, of those tiny capsules been launched into space on the off-chance that a few of them might land on a planet similar to their own and their cargo return to life in the body of a reasoning creature? Was that the purpose of the sign-writing and the geometric symbols? For millions of years the capsule must have drifted or lain unnoticed, but time was unimportant. The beings who had sent it out wished to become united with another intelligent race, and the symbols ensured that only a reasoning being would realize what the symbols meant and discover how to open it. Then the sharp spores would be released, the flesh of the host would be pierced and the take-over could commence.

'In a way, Miss Carlin, though, it is partly our own thought-processes that are at work against us.' Beck was pencilling a series of crosses on to the map. 'The organisms operate in a very beautiful manner. They not only absorb the human tissue, they unite with it, and incorporate every living cell into their own structure. The form and structure of the infected host changes, but is that so impossible to understand? One of the miracles of nature is how the chromosomes control the shape and growth of our bodies.

'Yes, that is how the enemy works: entrance, absorption and merger. Each time a victim is taken, more human brain tissue becomes united with the alien elements to wage war against its own race.

'Look at the map, Mr Wilde, and tell me if this does not show planning and intelligence.' He pointed to the crosses he had drawn. 'Here is Miss Carlin's house, here is where they found the farmer's belongings, here the postman's. This is the wood where Mrs Wallace was sunbathing. Here is the village where the thing appeared out of the drain.' Beck joined his crosses together to show a rigid, zigzagging line moving steadily towards Lanchester. 'You will also notice that only reasoning victims are selected and animals are ignored. The dead rats flushed out of the drain had been killed by the poison and showed no external injuries. The farmer's dog was unharmed.

'Excuse me, Dr Norseman, but we have to leave.' The Dean's housekeeper had appeared at the doorway. 'The police are clearing all this street now and there's an inspector at the door. He says everybody must be out of the house within five minutes at the latest.'

'Very well, Mrs Clarkson. You and your husband can take my car and we'll follow you in a moment.' He waved her aside, staring at the map obviously deep in thought, and then brought a fist down on the table.

'Don't you realize what you've just said, Beck? Don't you see that this is all we need?' His face beamed with relief and triumph. 'The creatures are following a definite course. We can work out where they are . . .'

'And all we need to do is to wait in ambush for them.' Beck shook his head. 'I am quite sure our friends are prepared for that and will have an answer to our defences. So far fungicides and insecticides appear useless against them and orthodox poisons have failed completely.

'What would you suggest, Mr Wilde?' It was John's turn to receive the look of pity. 'Bombs perhaps, a flame-thrower, artillery? The age of the vessel proves that it could not have had a human origin and it was without insulation. The spores would have been destroyed when it entered Earth's atmosphere if they had not been resistant to the most intense heat.'

'There must be a way, there has to be.' Mary took the Dean's place by the window. The queue to the station was shorter now and the traffic was thinning out. Soon Lanchester would be a deserted city waiting for the conquering army to take possession.

What controlled that army? she wondered. How did those creeping shapes gain the information to move so purposefully forward? Certainly not by sight or smell or hearing, but perhaps by a power that humanity had discarded and replaced with logic. Primitive man was thought to have possessed a sense of impending danger: an inborn warning device which deserted him when he discovered that fire and dogs and stockades were better methods of defence.

'There might have been a way, if we had been able to study the organism when it was weak. That was my ambition once and I am to blame for most of what has happened. When I saw that Railstone's corpse was mummified, I felt sure the cells must have atrophied, and I allowed Miss Leame and Marne to touch it.' Beck sounded completely indifferent as if the rout of humanity no longer concerned him. The Prussian general had accepted defeat and for him the war was over. He shook his head again as another helicopter rattled above the rooftops.

'I believed that if the organism had survived, it could have been used and controlled clinically, but now they will be so strong, so horribly strong.'

'What are you people doing here?' A harassed police inspector stood in the doorway. He had taken off his jacket and his shirt was dark with sweat. 'I gave orders that everybody must leave this area at once.'

'Why the sudden urgency, Inspector? I thought the evacuation was not to be completed till eight o'clock.' The Dean was still bent over the map. 'And please come over here for a moment. I think you should know that these . . . these creatures are advancing in a regular formation.'

'We know all about that, sir; do go to your car at once. The urgency is that we didn't realize the powers of the thing we are up against till a few minutes ago. Please don't argue with me, sir.' He frowned as Norseman made no move to obey him. 'Just get your party out of here while the going's good. The road is fairly clear till Stainwood, but there's a bad hold-up at the bridge and we want everybody across before nightfall. For God's sake do what you're told.' The inspector's face was drawn with fatigue and, as if in support of his plea, there came a long deep menacing rumble from the south.

★   ★   ★

They were almost at the end of the queue which moved slowly in fits and starts, and they never witnessed the panic and violence which developed when the bridge at Stainwood became completely blocked and fear turned into a living, personal thing. All the same it was a slow, anxious journey with the traffic crawling in three lanes and Mary's car jammed between a hearse packed tight with living bodies and a coach carrying 'walking' patients from the hospital.

John sat in the back with the Dean and he kept his eyes fixed on Erich Beck beside Mary. The German's face still appeared completely bleak; John tried to recall how he had looked on other occasions. The long hard stare when Mary had first mentioned the relic, the tension during the drive to her bungalow, the lack of surprise when Marne died. With every weary yard the memories returned to John and also some of the things Beck had said. 'Years ago I witnessed a very similar phenomenon.' That had been on the way to Caswell Hall. 'Banks and Marne may not have been isolated cases and Miss Carlin's relic may have had a double.' He had said that shortly before they reached the bungalow. 'I am the only person who really does know the nature of the threat that hangs over us.' He had made that claim to Brown just before the telephone rang and they learned that the vessel was not of human origin.

'Professor Beck, I think it is time that you put your cards on the table.' John leaned forward and gripped Beck's shoulder, feeling the slight body make no move to resist him. 'You keep implying that there is no defence against this organism and also that you have some personal knowledge of some earlier manifestation.' His fingers kneaded into the neck muscles, but though Beck gave a slight gasp of pain he still did not move. 'You will now tell us everything you know, Professor. The whole truth without any vague hints or concealment at all.'

'Most certainly, Mr Wilde, and there is no need for physical violence. I have been wanting to talk to someone for a very long time, but certain factors prevented me. Thank you.' He nodded gratefully as John released his grip.

'I have been a frightened man for very many years, and at last my fears have become unimportant. What do shame, disgrace or imprisonment matter compared to that horror behind us?' He turned and glanced back through the rear window and then at John and Norseman.

'Yes, Mr Wilde, you have every right to know the truth, and you are correct in believing that the tribunal should have found me guilty, Mr Dean. I am a criminal, I did visit Marienfeld camp, I do deserve to be punished.' He fiddled with his pipe and turned to Mary.

'You see, Miss Carlin, your supposed relic was not the only one to reach the earth. An identical object was discovered in Germany during the winter of 1943.'

Nineteen

CREDIT for unearthing the vessel found in Germany belonged to a unit of the R.A.F. A Halifax bomber, having failed to find its target and being separated from the rest of the squadron, was turning for home when flak knocked out its inner port engine. Because he was losing height, the pilot wisely decided to jettison his cargo and the bombs were released over open country, demolishing a barn and leaving six deep craters across a field of grazing land.

The capsule was noticed lying on the smoking earth and rubble by a farm labourer who contacted a nearby army unit, and the lieutenant who examined the thing considered it to be some form of anti-personnel device and a typical example of British frightful-ness. But his superior officer, a certain Major Lessing, took a very different view. The shape and general form of the vessel soon convinced him that it could not be a military weapon in the accepted sense of the word, and its engraved surface intrigued him greatly.

Though a professional soldier, Lessing was also a student of Norse mythology and the patterns suggested runes or mystical symbols to him. Was the object of antiquarian value perhaps? A *rimstock* or perpetual calendar which had lain buried in the field for centuries and dated far back beyond Christian times?

Knowing that both his Führer and Heinrich Himmler shared his hobby, Lessing contacted a relative at S.S. headquarters and in due course the object was sent to Berlin for detailed study.

'I never learned who finally deciphered the symbols or discovered how to open the vessel. I was living in Dresden at the time and did not come on the scene till some months later.' Beck puffed at his pipe while he told the story, and the convoy crawled and halted and then crawled on again in the retreat from Lanchester.

'It was in April, the last Sunday of the month, that Karl Fendel telephoned me. We had been students together and, though still a young man, he held the rank of S.S. colonel and was a close friend of Himmler. Fendel asked me about my own work at first; I was doing research on the nature of certain illnesses which appeared to increase mental activity; and then he told me that he was in charge of this establishment at Marienfeld where he had something of great interest to discuss with me.

'Fendel's car met me at the station and within a kilometre of the camp I knew what it was. First there was the stench of the place, then the huts spread out on a hillside in plain view of the road and the railway, then the guards and the dogs and the wire and the creatures behind the wire. But above all the stench. I can still smell that so-called research centre.' They stopped again, and Beck's pipe smoke drifted through the windows to join the exhaust fumes.

'Fendel took me round himself. He showed me everything that they had done: the induced tumours, the frost-bite cases, the men, women and children whose brains had been destroyed. And I did nothing. I made no protest, I did not even turn away. I walked beside Karl Fendel and I nodded as he pointed out the result of such and such an experiment and agreed that it was justified in the interests of science. I was a nonentity, you see, and he was a personal friend of Himmler's.' From under his glasses tears were trickling down Beck's cheeks.

'Then Fendel took me into a laboratory which was very heavily guarded. We talked about my own lines of research for a few minutes, and then he asked me to look into a microscope. The specimen on the slide was clearly organic, but resembled no chemical substance I had ever seen. When I shrugged and said that it meant nothing to me, he told me of the discovery of the capsule and that, in a Berlin lab, various animals had been treated with its contents and no apparent results had been recorded.'

'So, the remaining contents were sent to Marienfeld and human subjects were used?' Beck had broken off as if the memories were too painful, and the Dean prompted him.

'That is correct, Dr Norseman. Like Marne, Himmler was a visionary and the sign-writing on the capsule had convinced him that the stuff had magical properties. His friend, Karl Fendel, was the man who might discover what they were.

'I tried to hide my scepticism, but then Fendel led me into a room behind the laboratory which contained two metal cells with glass peep-holes, so that one could view their occupants in safety.' Beck had noticed his face in the driving mirror and he wiped the tears from his cheeks.

'There is no need for me to describe what the first cell contained, Miss Carlin. The occupant had been a Polish woman whom Fendel had infected shortly before my arrival. The other night outside your bungalow, you and Mr Wilde saw an identical being.

'But in the second cell, there was something wonderful: a little Jewish boy who smiled and talked to us through a microphone. He had been in poor health when he was treated, but within hours of the infection he was physically recovered. But there was more to it than that – much more. The child was of average intelligence, but his I.Q. had multiplied at least three times, and he showed definite proof of genius.' Until a moment ago Beck had looked crushed by guilt, but now there was both excitement and anger in his expression.

'If only that boy had been allowed to live, we could have learned so much from him. Perhaps we might even have harnessed the organism and used it to produce a super race. That is why when, years later, I heard of Railstone's career and the legends of the relic, I wondered if his had been a similar phenomenon.'

'They killed the boy?' John had been taking shorthand notes and he looked up with a jerk. 'What about the woman?'

'They killed her too, Mr Wilde. The same evening three senior S.S. officials arrived at the camp to inspect Fendel's progress. They took one look at the woman, or rather what she had become; already she was unrecognizable as a human being and, without even examining the boy, they ordered Fendel to destroy both subjects.

'The fools! The ignorant frightened fools. There was no danger, the creatures were in sealed containers, the very air they exhaled was filtered.' Beck was watching a flight of reconnaissance planes zigzagging across the downs. 'Fendel and I pleaded that the boy be allowed to live, but they were adamant and their credentials were signed by Himmler.'

'But how were they destroyed?' Mary had understood John's excitement. 'You have kept telling us that there is no defence because the organism is virtually indestructible.'

'Because we lack the means, Miss Carlin. Before the spores become united with living tissue, several chemicals can kill them. After they are established, however, there is only one way to touch them.' The planes had vanished beyond the horizon and he lowered his head and stared at the floor of the car.

'A "wedding of opposites" was how Karl Fendel described his method. Remember that the subjects were unrelated and they still retained human anti-bodies. They also possessed alien defence organisms whose nature had been influenced by their separate metabolisms. Karl was a clever scientist, we have to grant him that, and what he did was so simple and practical. He merely removed the partition between the compartments and allowed the creatures to come together. The two strains attempted to merge but

they rejected each other. The genes could not fuse and within seconds we saw that they were degenerating. In less than five minutes
they were both dead.

'Why talk about it? The organism can absorb all human tissue
not infected by itself, and there is nothing to be done. If some of
the original spores were obtainable, if we could find a volunteer
willing to turn himself into a living bomb, a human serum, then
Karl's "wedding" might take place again. But Railstone emptied
the vessel and the possibility does not exist.'

'That may not be true.' The convoy had begun to crawl forward,
but Mary did not follow the vehicle in front of her. She waited for
the coach to pass and then drove straight over the kerb.

'We might still be able to do something.' She reversed the car
and pointed its bonnet towards Lanchester. 'Have you all forgotten
the other vessel which was left in the tomb of Abbot Vulfrum?'

*   ★   ⋆

'That is settled then. We go back to the cathedral.' With the prospect that some action might be taken, they all felt strangely elated
and Beck rubbed his hands together while Mary waited for the tail
of the convoy to pass.

'Good, clever girl, to remember that. If the second half of the
capsule is still in the tomb, if it contains spores and was not merely
a propellant, if we can remove the stopper in time, then there is
a chance. A slight one, but at least we will be doing something
instead of waiting to be destroyed.'

'Have you people broken down?' An army lorry drew up and a
corporal leaned out of the cab. 'We can take the four of you at a
pinch, so hop in the back and please be quick about it.'

'No, corporal, our car is all right, but we do need your help.'
Norseman got out of the car and hobbled over to him. 'It is essential we return to Lanchester at once, and I want you to come with
us. Tell your driver to turn round.'

'Back there, with them devils on the move?' The soldier's mouth
had dropped open and he goggled at Norseman, as if unable to
believe his own ears. From the back of the truck a walkie-talkie

was reviewing the situation. 'Evacuation of the municipal area is now complete. Units in Squares 3, 5 and 6 are to withdraw to their second positions. All other units are to wait for further orders, but withdraw at once if any enemy activity occurs in their areas. Repeat. Units in . . .'

'Yes, back there, corporal, and jump to it.' Norseman watched the last retreating vehicles crawl past with police motorcyclists bringing up the rear. They looked incuriously at the parked car, obviously thinking that the army would take care of its occupants.

'Sorry, sir, but you must be barmy. They keep talking about those things as the *enemy* because they can't think of a better word.' The soldier craned further out of the cab and stared down the empty road. 'But I've spoken to blokes who've actually seen 'em. There's nothing we can do to stop them at the moment. In the morning the air force is going to try napalm and we're to get the hell out of here. Now, for Christ's sake go back to your car and follow us.'

'I am not barmy, corporal. Until recently I was a ranking army officer and I am giving you an order.' Norseman might have sounded impressive if his voice had not been drowned by a roar of exhaust as the driver let in his clutch and the lorry lumbered away to rejoin the retreat.

'Very well. We're on our own then, but not to worry.' He climbed back into the car and Mary edged it over the kerb and accelerated down the road. 'The four of us are going to lick this thing without any help from anybody.' Norseman smiled at Erich Beck. Though Beck's confession of what he had seen at Marienfeld revolted him, they were allies for the time being and the past was best forgotten.

It was a lovely evening, very much like the one on which Bishop Renton had died: the sunlight dappling the rolling countryside, little flat clouds in the sky and the cathedral towers like the sails of a ship coming hull up as the roof of the nave rose into sight.

'Yes, we might do it. If we can break into the tomb and find the container, if the spores are there, and you can take them to a laboratory in London, then there is a chance.' Beck was still massaging his hands and staring down at the floor of the car. 'And I, my friends, will at last have done something to justify what I witnessed at Marienfeld and did not dare to speak about.

'Ah, perhaps these soldiers may help us.' He looked up as Mary braked. Beyond a sharp curve, the road was blocked by two more army lorries. The bonnet of one of them was open and an officer and the driver were bent over the engine, while the men in the back of the trucks appeared stunned or completely exhausted.

'What's that?' The officer did not raise his head when Norseman approached him. 'No one's supposed to be in this area, so just obey orders, and turn round. We'll follow you as soon as we've cleared this fuel line.

'Go to Lanchester with you? With respect, sir, you must be out of your mind. Ask those chaps what happened and let us get on with our work.'

Though it was barely five minutes before the fuel pipe was cleared and the lorries left, they learned a great deal from the soldiers.

John and Norseman had not been the only people to realize the enemy were moving in formation and consider heat and explosives to be the obvious defence against them. Field guns with incendiary projectiles and supported by flame-throwers had been positioned on a ridge five miles to the south of Lanchester and the explosions they heard in the Dean's study had marked one stage of the battle. Each man used different terms to describe what had happened, but the facts were completely clear. The result had been rout followed by panic.

'They put us at the end of a big field, miss,' a white-faced corporal told Mary. 'The ground was still damp after all that rain and it steamed in the sun. All a bit of a lark we thought the exercise was, and Captain Giles let us smoke when the guns were in position and loaded. After all, what had we got to shoot at? So quiet and peaceful everything was at first.'

'I can't describe it properly like.' John had been questioning a young private. 'I was almost half asleep when I heard the officer in charge of the flame-thrower units blow a whistle and they all started forward. Then, when they were about halfway down the slope, Harry Wilson over there grips my arm and says "Christ! The bloody grass is standing up."'

'That's what it looked like, anyway.' Wilson was giving his version to Beck. 'The field was damp and all beaten down by the rain and then the whole of the far end seemed to rear up like a wave and start rolling towards our chaps.' Wilson's account was the most coherent and it was exactly what Beck had expected to hear. He could picture that slow unhurried ripple across the field, the soldiers halting, raising the nozzles of their weapons and the great gusts of flame fanning out, igniting the damp vegetation and scorching the earth itself. But *Nuber Caswellensis* had ignored them. The ripple had continued through the flames and over the charred, smoking earth and the blackened stubble. It had moved in a half-moon formation a few feet high, perhaps a hundred yards deep and two hundred from one crescent to the other, and the thing neither slackened nor increased speed as it approached the soldiers. Then one by one the flamethrowers were extinguished, the more intelligent ran and the brave crumpled like slashed sawdust dolls.

The artillery had opened up at that moment. Firing at their lowest elevation the three guns pounded the field, the phosphorus charges increasing the fires and acrid smoke obscuring visibility. Then the first gun had fallen silent, then the second and Wilson's crew saw that they were both unmanned, though fragments of khaki uniforms were being carried forward as the wave moved steadily on towards them. The battle ended abruptly.

'We just ran for the truck, miss, and I don't care what anybody says about us,' the corporal kept repeating to Mary. 'If you'd seen that stuff moving, seen the way the lads crumpled up as it reached them, you wouldn't blame us. And the stench of the things. Even with the smoke and the phosphorus we could smell the bastards.' At that moment the fuel line had been cleared, the officer made his last appeal and the lorries drove off.

'A battle has been lost, as Marne said, but this gives me hope.' Beck had remained silent for a while and the car was already approaching the centre of Lanchester. 'Though we know that orthodox weapons are useless, we have learned something else. Those creatures are quite definitely on their way to the cathedral and their mission must be the same as ours. They know that the second section of the capsule contains their own sporified tissue and that it can be both an ally and the one thing which can destroy them.'

'Drive right up to the front entrance please. I gave orders that the main door remain unlocked, though don't ask me why. Sanctuary for stragglers, perhaps.' The Dean looked at his watch as the car drew up before the porch.

'I would suggest that you stay here and keep a look-out, Mary. If the creatures' rate of progress does not alter we should have almost a full hour before they make an appearance. Ample time to find what we are looking for and get the hell out of here, as the vulgar say.' With physical action in sight, Norseman obviously considered he should assume command. 'I hope your muscles are in good working order, gentlemen, so let's get started.' He stepped out of the car and moved slowly but purposefully towards the doorway.

The electricity had been cut off, the sun had begun to go down, but candles and the coloured beams from the stained-glass windows gave them adequate light. They collected tools from the verger's store-room first, then walked up through the long nave with their footsteps echoing in the silence of the deserted building; up past the famous figure-of-eight screen with its bas-reliefs illustrating episodes of St Paul's ministry, up through the dark choir stalls leading towards the high altar, till finally they came to the tomb of Vulfrum.

The abbot's effigy lay stretched out on a stone dais with hands composed in prayer, and a small animal, perhaps a dog or a cat, was crouched at his feet. The marble face was smooth and noseless, but traces of lips remained and they were smiling.

'Are we mad? Is this the way to stop them?' Beck had insisted on taking the first turn with the pick, and John kept asking himself the question as the small energetic figure chipped away at the side of the tomb. When Beck had told them what had happened in Germany, and Mary had remembered the existence of the second vessel, he had been hopeful. But, as the blows of the pick rang out, the stone mouth of Vulfrum sneered at him and, from the windows, the faces of angels and saints and patriarchs appeared sad and pitying. Perhaps the second orb had also been stolen at some later date, perhaps it was empty, and even if the spores existed and they got them to London, who would volunteer to provide the living bomb Beck had so glibly suggested?

'Your turn, Mr Wilde. Try to cut through the base and the right-hand side now.' Beck had already completed an 'L'-shaped groove round two edges of the panel and he handed John the axe. 'The capsule must be there, just beyond the panel and waiting for us. I know it, I can sense it, I am sure of it. Not a separate vessel as we once thought, but the second compartment of one missile which divided when it reached the earth's surface.

'Good, good, Wilde. You should be through in a moment and, if your estimate is correct, Dr Norseman, you will be on your way back to London before the creatures even reach the outskirts of Lanchester. But first I must find how to release the stopper.' The slab shuddered loosely under John's blows, and Beck picked up a crowbar.

'There, that should give us enough room.' John had stepped back and he inserted the bar into the cut. 'Use the pickaxe as a lever now, and you help me to bear down on the bar, Dr Norseman.

'Ah yes, it is giving. The stone is coming away.' They all gasped with their exertions, but slowly and reluctantly, like an obstinate tooth being torn from its socket, the heavy panel rumbled away from the tomb. Behind lay folds of cloth which time had shrivelled as fine as cobwebs, a heap of old, brown bones, and the thing that they had prayed to find. The stopper was still in position and the orb gleamed as brightly as its fellow had done in the Caswell vaults.

Twenty

SEVEN o'clock. High over the tree tops, Old Tom boomed out the hour and in the silence his notes sounded loud enough to wake the dead. As the cliché occurred to her, Mary's sense of loneliness increased because, in a sense, it was true. For fifteen million years the dead had slept, but now they were awake and on the move.

How much longer would John and the others be? Mary was

standing beside the car with the deserted town spread out around her. To the right lay Queen's Crescent, a regency terrace designed by Nash and almost as great a source of pride to the inhabitants of Lanchester as the cathedral. Beyond the Crescent, the concrete blocks of the university towered arrogantly above the older buildings, while straight ahead the High Street with its motley collection of half-timbered pubs, bingo halls and chain stores stretched away to the railway bridge. The sun was still bright upon the pretentious dome of the station and beyond the bridge, though out of sight, was a roundabout and the road to Kentham – the route along which the invaders might be approaching.

Even if the chalice existed and they found that it contained the spores, could Beck's plan possibly stop them? Mary still kept thinking of the objects by the term *chalice*. After all, Beck had been a witness to the earlier destruction, not its architect.

How genuine had been Beck's show of remorse, if it came to that? Mary tried to imagine what might have gone on in his mind since those days at Marienfeld. He had confessed to guilt, but also admitted intense curiosity, talking of the Jewish boy's death not as murder, but as a loss to science. He had also believed that the alien genus could have been beneficially merged with the human to produce a superior race.

Then Beck had learned about Railstone's sudden burst of genius and his dream had returned, becoming an obsession which had allowed him to ignore the dangers involved, while fear of facing a second arrest had kept him quiet till it was too late.

Or might Beck have been lying about his remorse? Had he been, not a visitor to the camp, but an active member of its staff? Certainly his suggestion of using a human bait to destroy *Nuber Caswellensis* implied complete callousness. Mary shivered as another thought occurred to her: was the man insane, perhaps, or possessed by the kind of powers that Norseman feared? Had his fascination with the organism completely turned his mind, and did he intend, not the salvation of the human race, but its destruction? Did he hope to strengthen the creature with the contents of the second chalice and hasten the *Götterdämmerung*?

No, whatever Beck was – a fanatic, a dedicated Nazi – they had to trust him, because even the most evil human being could not wish for the success of the thing which was coming. Mary recalled Nancy Leame's lion-faced features staring at her and how her half-human voice had muttered from behind the kitchen door. That floating or crawling carpet was not just an enemy to be resisted, not merely one species fighting for survival at the expense of another. The alien strain in Railstone's body had given him arche-typal memories of what the beings which possessed him had been like, and his paintings had shown figures which were outlandish and inhuman, but definitely individual. They had hoped for sur-vival and failed. The mutant to which Nancy Leame had given birth was an obscenity that bore small resemblance to either of the races which had produced it.

'Little Boy Blue come blow your horn,
The sheep's in the meadow, the cow's in the corn.'

The tune she had heard just before she turned and saw Nancy swaying before her ran through Mary's mind, and she hummed to keep herself company. Clouds were gathering in the south and, along the opposite pavement, two cats slunk like shadows. Behind them, nose to the ground, body drooped dejectedly, came a black mongrel, obviously in search of its owners.

'Here, boy. Come to me, there's a good boy.' The dog trotted over when Mary called, and she reached out and fondled its ears, gaining companionship from the prod of a friendly nose, but none from the shivering body and stricken eyes. Twenty minutes had passed since they had reached the cathedral and Norseman must have been guessing when he estimated there was a clear hour before them. In the distance another helicopter was circling the town. The soldiers had said that napalm bombs would be used in the morning, but phosphorus and flame-throwers had already been tried and proved worthless.

'No, boy, stay here.' The clock struck the quarter and the dog whimpered and drew back. 'Please stay with me, darling.' Mary reached for the collar, but the mongrel growled and then bounded away up the street as if a leopard were at its heels. As she watched it go she noticed that there was not a bird to be seen and that she was completely alone.

Not for long, however, because more refugees were on the way. Mary turned, hearing a strange medley of noises and saw a clanking, clattering, bellowing army emerge from under the railway bridge and come hurrying towards her.

A big Hereford bull with barbed wire clinging to his horns and withers led the way, and a herd of cows, bullocks and heifers were at his heels. Behind the cattle came three horses and an old shaggy donkey, followed by a jostling rabble of sheep and pigs, and a rearguard of assorted poultry; all squawking and flapping their wings in desperation to keep up with the leaders. Rank by ragged rank they hurried past to vanish finally over the brow of the hill. The invaders were only thought to attack human beings, but the animals were obviously terrified of them, and Mary remembered her own feelings as she had sat at the desk with the chalice before her. Awe and reverence slowly turned to revulsion as she realized that she was not examining any holy thing, but an object of menace.

Seven thirty already. If the second vessel did exist, surely they must have found it by now. Loud and menacing the notes rang out, and the sun was going down fast, dusk obscuring the distant hills and turning the dome of the railway station blue-black. Beneath the bridge more animals were on their way: she could see them pouring through the arches. They were moving very slowly this time and, though half a mile distant, it was strange that she did not hear them.

No, what she saw were not animals, but only shadows projected by the setting sun. Shadows so broad that the street could not contain them, and their vast shapes bulged up over the buildings as if coating their walls with fur. Shadows which brought the same smell she had experienced in the bungalow, and which were moving in an opposite direction to the sun.

'John, John darling!' Mary ran through the cathedral door and the organ pipes echoed her cries back to her. 'John, Professor, Dr Norseman! Hurry! They are here already. I have seen them.'

'How far away, Miss Carlin?' Beck was standing before the candles on the high altar with his back to the rifled tomb. 'By the railway bridge? Good. You still have a few minutes then.' His gloved hands replaced the stopper of the orb and wiped its surface on the altar cloth.

'Remember what I told you, gentlemen. Explain the time factors, temperatures and rate of growth to the authorities. Above all, impress on them that the remaining contents of this vessel is the only defence they have. It will be up to them to find a volunteer to man the weapon.' He turned with a slight smile, handed the orb to John and then bent over the altar again.

'But you had better go at once. You have checked that the back doors are locked and the only way out is by the front. Besides, the car is directly in the path of the creatures, so please hurry. Goodbye to you all.

'What are you waiting for?' Beck had been examining a smear of greyish matter he had laid on the altar stone and he swung round angrily when Norseman touched his arm. 'I have said goodbye, so don't just stand there. Go while you have the chance.'

'We are waiting for you, Professor. Aren't you coming?'

'God! You fool, Norseman. Haven't you understood a single word I said? Of course I am not leaving with you.' He pulled off his gloves and reached for something in his pocket. 'Don't you realize that each minute, each second that passes is giving the organism added strength and resistance? Don't you see that I have to stay here and hit it now, at once?' A penknife glinted under the candles and before they could stop him Beck had slashed his left wrist and was kneading the greyish matter into the wound.

'A theatrical gesture, because we know that the spores can penetrate unbroken skin. But it must convince you that there is nothing you can do to help me, and I am already a part of the enemy. Get out and take that container to London.' He stamped his foot as they made no move to obey him.

'Try to understand that I am not being heroic. It is simply that I have a debt to pay. I saw what was happening at Marienfeld, but I stood aside like the crowd on Calvary and made no protest. Then, years later, when I suspected what Railstone's tomb contained, the dream of controlling the organism scientifically, of harnessing it, became a mania. Finally, even after I realized what a monster we had set free, the fear of facing another tribunal kept me quiet till it was too late.'

High above them a trapped bird fluttered against the windows and another smell had started to join the church odours of incense, polished woodwork and candle smoke.

'Oh, the things I saw at Marienfeld! The results of the experiments they showed me! Since that day I have lived in a hell and only the hope of finding that organism and harnessing it for our general good kept me from suicide. I dreamed of producing a superior race and all I have done is to release a blight upon the earth.' Beck's face looked tortured, but his hand was quite steady as he raised it to show the stuff clinging to his wrist.

'Surely I have the right to repay my debt alone?'

'Yes, that is your right.' Norseman gave a stiff bow. 'And I think I can make a promise, Professor Beck. Whatever you have done in the past, God has forgiven you now.' He turned, motioned John and Mary to follow him, and started to walk down to the chancel. On the second step he halted and his body became as rigid as the statue on Vulfrum's tomb. Through the choir and the carved screen, beyond the organ and the long nave, they could see that their escape had been cut off and *Nuber Caswellensis* was already with them.

The door was open and while Beck had made his appeal the enemy had come pouring in. No low, nebulous cloud or carpet, but a vast, swollen mass which glistened like wet leather in the fading light; a rolling wave of bloated tissue that changed its form while it moved through the church, as though the thing were some monstrous amoeba avoiding obstacles or wrapping itself around victims. Spear-heads like hands clutched at walls and pillars to drag the main body forward, tentacles slid over benches and tore them aside to give it headway. Slowly and without hurry the organism came on. But worse than the sight and the smell of the thing were the sounds it made.

Sobs and gasps and chattering noises came first. Moans as if each yard covered was done so in intense agony. But finally all the sounds merged into a myriad gasping whispering voices that issued orders and made a promise.

Obedience was what the voices demanded. Let there be complete submission and the promise would be kept. There would be no more fear, no more pain, no more death: the only price was acceptance and surrender. Louder and louder the voices became and they all heard them clearly: Norseman and John and Mary, who had drawn back to the altar, and Erich Beck who had walked down the steps and was standing alone on the chancel floor. They never knew whether telepathy or a physical force transmitted those gasping words of command, but they came from every corner of the cathedral and were repeated over and over again by the organ pipes, the statues and the faces in the stained-glass windows. Even the tortured figure on the crucifix appeared to be pleading for obedience while the glistening mass spread from one wall of the building to the other and its spear-heads flowed towards the tomb of Vulfrum.

John laid the metal orb on the altar and took Mary in his arms, while the Dean stood stiffly beside them. They knew there was no escape by running away and all they could do was to stand there and wait for the thing that was approaching; smelling the stench of burned garlic, listening to its voices, feeling the whole fabric of the cathedral tremble with its pressure and weight. A mass composed of millions of tiny individuals acting together, or one unit? A new creation or something immensely old which had been revived in a different form? Even as Erich Beck went to his end, John considered that.

The spear-heads were into the choir and streaming towards the chancel when Beck moved to meet them. He glanced back at the group by the altar and then walked across to the shattered tomb and stationed himself before the breach, with his shoulders drawn back and his head held high. He smiled at two mottled tentacles gliding across the floor and he nodded at a long glistening arm as though he were greeting an old friend. Then the arm and the tentacles joined together, reared up and reached out to make an end of him.

Beck went. Much of his life had been governed by fear and guilt and curiosity: now he had gone to his dream. He was simply there one instant and then not there. He shrank, withered, vanished and was gone. Fragments of clothing clung to the wave that had swallowed him, but there was no sign of the man himself, nothing left of him, nothing to show he had ever existed. The mass poured over the tomb, halted for a moment and then started to flow towards the altar steps.

'Don't look at it and don't let the voices hypnotize you. Get on your knees and try to pray.' Norseman was a sick man, but by brute force he pulled them down. The nearest tentacles were halfway across the chancel when John and Mary turned their faces to the altar.

' "Our Father which art in Heaven . . ." ' The Dean's voice resisted the words of command, but the garlic smell grew stronger and stronger till they felt as if they were being smothered by a gas compressed into a liquid.

' "Hallowed be Thy Name . . . Thy Kingdom come . . ." ' Inch by inch the mass was moving across the floor and towards the altar steps, and Mary waited for its touch on her body. She knew there was no point in physical resistance and all she could do was to accept whatever fate offered.

' "Thy Will be done . . ." ' Were the voices changing in some way as they drew nearer? Had they become weaker? Mary looked at the metal orb on the altar and once again she saw it gleam as the other had done in the Caswell vaults. She closed her eyes and pressed her face against John's.

' "In Earth as it is in Heaven . . ." ' At that moment John knew hope, because Norseman's voice sounded much louder and the other voices were faltering. The commands were becoming incoherent and changing to meaningless sentences, disjointed phrases, unconnected words. Then there were no words at all; only a series of gasps and sobs followed by a dry rustling sound as if feet were trampling through dead leaves.

John was the first to turn round and, even in the deep gloom, one glance told him that Erich Beck had paid his debt and Norseman's faith had triumphed. The spores had turned his human cells into a serum and they were destroying the alien tissue which had absorbed them.

Stuff, dying stuff, was falling from the walls and pillars, and stuff was the only word to describe it. Harmless stuff without strength and vitality crumbling on the pews and the benches. Clouds of stuff drifting like cobwebs in the air. Dead stuff cracking and withering and drying on the floor.

Conclusion

WITHIN forty-eight hours life started to return to normal, though it took several weeks to clear Lanchester cathedral of the acrid dust which clung to its interior, and much longer before the Cass reservoir was free of the copper sulphate that had tinted its waters a delicate shade of blue. The second half of the vessel was never reopened, but lowered into the depths of the Atlantic, securely enclosed in a lead cocoon.

Shortly after Christmas John and Mary were married by the Dean, while before Easter Norseman had concluded his celebrated quarrel with the new bishop, who still bears traces of a broken nose, and been dispatched to Central Africa in disgrace. He now rules the diocese of M'Shimbaville with a very heavy hand.

The final act did not take place till almost a year later, when a royal personage unveiled a statue in the cathedral precincts and a plaque which read 'To the memory and example of Erich Beck who died as he had lived in the service of mankind.'

Flowers and wreaths are always to be found beside that statue and once a year the mayor adds the city's official tribute. The inhabitants of Lanchester derive both pride and profit from its presence, since from all over the world visitors flock to pay their respects and purchase silver-gilt medallions embossed with their saviour's likeness.

Norseman and the Wildes kept Beck's secret well and humanity never discovered that it owed its continued existence to a self-confessed war criminal.

JOHN BLACKBURN (1923-1993)
Photo by Laura Richardson, Weston, Mass.
(From the dust jacket of the 1962 American edition of *Broken Boy*)

NEW & FORTHCOMING TITLES FROM VALANCOURT BOOKS

R. C. ASHBY (RUBY FERGUSON)	He Arrived at Dusk
FRANK BAKER	The Birds
WALTER BAXTER	Look Down in Mercy
CHARLES BEAUMONT	The Hunger and other Stories
DAVID BENEDICTUS	The Fourth of June
PAUL BINDING	Harmonica's Bridegroom
JOHN BLACKBURN	A Scent of New-Mown Hay
	Broken Boy
	Blue Octavo
	Nothing But the Night
	Bury Him Darkly
	The Household Traitors
	Our Lady of Pain
	A Beastly Business
THOMAS BLACKBURN	The Feast of the Wolf
JOHN BRAINE	Room at the Top
	The Vodi
BASIL COPPER	The Great White Space
	Necropolis
RONALD FRASER	Flower Phantoms
STEPHEN GILBERT	The Burnaby Experiments
CLAUDE HOUGHTON	I Am Jonathan Scrivener
	This Was Ivor Trent
FRANCIS KING	To the Dark Tower
	Never Again
	An Air that Kills
	The Dividing Stream
	The Dark Glasses
	The Man on the Rock
C.H.B. KITCHIN	Ten Pollitt Place
	The Book of Life
HILDA LEWIS	The Witch and the Priest
KENNETH MARTIN	Aubade
	Waiting for the Sky to Fall

MICHAEL MCDOWELL	The Amulet
MICHAEL NELSON	Knock or Ring
	A Room in Chelsea Square
BEVERLEY NICHOLS	Crazy Pavements
OLIVER ONIONS	The Hand of Kornelius Voyt
DENNIS PARRY	Sea of Glass
ROBERT PHELPS	Heroes and Orators
J.B. PRIESTLEY	Benighted
	The Other Place
FORREST REID	The Garden God
	The Tom Barber Trilogy
	At the Door of the Gate
	The Spring Song
HENRY DE VERE STACPOOLE	The Blue Lagoon
JOHN TREVENA	Furze the Cruel
	Sleeping Waters
JOHN WAIN	Hurry on Down
	The Smaller Sky
HUGH WALPOLE	The Killer and the Slain
KEITH WATERHOUSE	There is a Happy Land
	Billy Liar
ALEC WAUGH	The Loom of Youth
COLIN WILSON	Ritual in the Dark
	The Philosopher's Stone

Selected Eighteenth and Nineteenth Century Classics

ANONYMOUS	Teleny
	The Sins of the Cities of the Plain
GRANT ALLEN	Miss Cayley's Adventures
JOANNA BAILLIE	Six Gothic Dramas
EATON STANNARD BARRETT	The Heroine
WILLIAM BECKFORD	Azemia
COUNTESS OF BLESSINGTON	Marmaduke Herbert
MARY ELIZABETH BRADDON	Thou Art the Man
JOHN BUCHAN	Sir Quixote of the Moors
HALL CAINE	The Manxman
MONA CAIRD	The Wing of Azrael

EMILY FLYGARE-CARLÉN	The Magic Goblet
MARY CHOLMONDELEY	Diana Tempest
MARIE CORELLI	The Sorrows of Satan
	Ziska
CAROLINE CLIVE	Paul Ferroll
BARON CORVO	Stories Toto Told Me
	Hubert's Arthur
GABRIELE D'ANNUNZIO	The Intruder (L'innocente)
JOHN DAVIDSON	Earl Lavender
THOMAS DE QUINCEY	Klosterheim
ARTHUR CONAN DOYLE	The Parasite
	Round the Red Lamp
BARON DE LA MOTTE FOUQUÉ	Zeluco
SARAH GRAND	Ideala
H. RIDER HAGGARD	Nada the Lily
ERNEST G. HENHAM	Tenebrae
CHARLES JOHNSTONE	Chrysal (2 vols)
CAROLINE LAMB	Glenarvon
FRANCIS LATHOM	The Castle of Ollada
	The Midnight Bell
	The Fatal Vow
	Astonishment!!!
	The One-Pound Note
	The Impenetrable Secret
	The Mysterious Freebooter
SOPHIA LEE	The Two Emilys
SHERIDAN LE FANU	Carmilla
	The Cock and Anchor
	The Rose and the Key
M. G. LEWIS	The Monk
ELIZA LYNN LINTON	Realities
EDWARD BULWER LYTTON	Eugene Aram
FLORENCE MARRYAT	The Blood of the Vampire
	There is no Death
RICHARD MARSH	The Beetle
	The Goddess: A Demon
	A Spoiler of Men
	The Seen and the Unseen

	Both Sides of the Veil
	Curios
	A Second Coming
	Philip Bennion's Death
	The Complete Sam Briggs Stories
	The Complete Judith Lee Stories
BERTRAM MITFORD	Renshaw Fanning's Quest
	The Sign of the Spider
	The Weird of Deadly Hollow
	The King's Assegai
	The White Shield
	The Induna's Wife
JOHN MOORE	Zeluco
OUIDA	Under Two Flags
	In Maremma
ELIZA PARSONS	Castle of Wolfenbach
	The Mysterious Warning
WALTER PATER	Marius the Epicurean
ROSA PRAED	Fugitive Anne
FRANCIS PREVOST	Rust of Gold
ANN RADCLIFFE	The Italian
	The Mysteries of Udolpho
	Gaston de Blondeville
CLARA REEVE	The Old English Baron
GEORGE W.M. REYNOLDS	The Mysteries of London
	The Necromancer
REGINA MARIA ROCHE	The Children of the Abbey
	Clermont
JAMES MALCOLM RYMER	The Black Monk
PERCY BYSSHE SHELLEY	The Cenci
M. P. SHIEL	Prince Zaleski
CHARLOTTE SMITH	The Story of Henrietta
BRAM STOKER	The Watter's Mou'
	The Mystery of the Sea
	Lady Athlyne
	The Lady of the Shroud
	The Snake's Pass

CPSIA information can be obtained at www.ICGtesting.com
Printed in the USA
LVOW07s2152230913

353797LV00009B/257/P

9 781939 140173